When Cassie's family moves into a decrepit house in New Orleans, the only upside is her new best friend. Gem is witty, attractive, and sure not to abandon Cassie—after all, she's been confined to the old house since her murder in the '60s.

As their connection becomes romantic, Cassie must keep more and more secrets from her religious community, which hates ghosts almost as much as it hates gays. Even if their relationship prevails over volatile parents and brutal conversion therapy, it may not outlast time.

# THE WOMEN OF

# DAUPHINE

*Deb Jannerson*

A NineStar Press Publication

Published by NineStar Press
P.O. Box 91792,
Albuquerque, New Mexico, 87199 USA.
www.ninestarpress.com

# The Women of Dauphine

Printed in the USA
First Edition
June, 2019

Print ISBN: 978-1-950412-89-1

Also available in eBook, ISBN: 978-1-950412-88-4

Warning: This book contains sexual content, which may only be suitable for mature readers, and scenes of violence and references to child abuse and suicide.

For the queer teens of the 1990s,
and for the queer teens of today

# Prologue

"SAY IT AGAIN, miss."

"She's not real."

"And again!"

But I had begun crying by then. I imagined her next to my chair, staring in betrayal, her eyelids half lowered. In my groggy mind, it seemed possible she could be witnessing this scene, that the laws of space could bend to bring her to her Judas. The word tore itself out of my mouth: "No."

He hit the switch, and I writhed as electricity infused my body. I saw spots that became blotches and covered my vision, before the warm-up second ended and I saw nothing at all. When I went still, Dr. Salamander lowered himself to my level, no more than several feet away, and searched my face.

"The conclusion?"

I pushed myself to gather my breath, which just made me panic more. His finger strayed toward the switch again, and my voice appeared.

"There's no such thing as a ghost."

# PART ONE

# Chapter One

I MET GEM the day we moved from the sedate suburbs to downtown New Orleans.

I had recently turned eight, and my first sight of her coincided with our first sight of the Victorian house. I'm not certain if some of my earliest memories are authentic or recreated by photos and hearsay, but that moment made for a striking mental snapshot I've never doubted: baroque, crumbling pink-and-ivory walls; a stylish teenaged 1960s brunette perched on the steps. I feasted my eyes upon her in the way only a curious child can. The opportunity delighted me, especially because my parents had forbidden me to stare at the young runaways clogging the sidewalk. The *lost children*.

I'd be leery of any Crescent City-raised kid who claimed never to have been fascinated by them. The lost children of the city streets were as diverse in origin as they were in countenance. The first I'd seen that morning had been a tap-dancing boy around my own age, gleefully calling to various "cutie-pahs" in an undetermined accent. His joy reached out to me, undisturbed by the morning's sharp tang of whiskey and street cleaner. I might not have believed he was alone in the world, like the poor souls my parents derided, if not for the layers of sweat marks on his clothes. My parents ignored his dollar-filled top hat and turned my head away in an admonishment. This made me wonder, maybe for the first time, what kind of people they were.

Then, I saw the girl: late teens, stringy sandy hair like frayed rope, weeping with abandon without bothering to hide her face from the tourists and blue-collar shop workers. She seemed "lost," all right; certainly, more so than the cartoon boys of *Peter Pan* who had introduced me to the "lost" term in the first place. I remembered the twitch in my father's face as he snapped the TV's power button in one fluid motion and turned to explain who the *lost children* of Louisiana really were.

The girl waiting at our dwelling on Dauphine Street shared a hint of the blonde crier's defiance, but she also exuded fun. She didn't bother to sit in the ladylike way I'd learned in church. Still, she jumped up before I reached an angle at which I could see up her green skirt—a fact I noted matter-of-factly, and with some vague sense of disappointment. I continued to examine her clothes anyway, with a youth's comically bobbing head. I had never seen tights like that before; they were nothing but strings in a diamond pattern. And was that a Boy Scout shirt?

"Hi!" I yelled, unnecessarily since we were barely five feet apart by now. There were chuckles behind me; it seemed like my parents always laughed at me doing normal, serious things. The girl staggered backward, widening her brown-gold eyes. "What's your name?" She glanced at my parents in something like panic, then back at me, and her face softened.

"I'm Gem." She glanced behind me again, and I followed her gaze to my mother, situated behind the battered chain-link fence, gazing blankly at our narrow new house. My father caught up, breaking through her reverie as he bustled through the space where a gate should be and pulled our keys out of his suit pocket.

The girl—Gem—stumbled off the stairs and several steps to the right, which is to say, at the edge of the property. Her eyes followed my parents carefully as they entered our new home. Obviously, I didn't know it at the time, but she was waiting to see if they'd notice her as I had.

Perhaps all houses came with a pretty girl, or maybe she was moving out. "Dad, can Gem come inside?"

My mother turned around in the corridor first. "What, Cassandra?"

"Can she come in with me?" I pointed at Gem and then grabbed her hand. She made a short sound of surprise at my touch.

My mother rolled her eyes elaborately. It didn't take much to annoy her, especially where I was concerned. She turned to my father, hissing, "Isn't she a bit old for this?" I could hear the disgust.

My father, unusually jovial today, held up a hand, and my mother went quiet. "It's okay." To me: "Sure, little one. Let's all go in and look around."

Gem's expression had gone both stunned and amused. It was a face I'd come to know well and love: the face of a person thrust into a strange scenario she was more than game enough to explore.


"YOU NEVER TOLD me your name." Gem flopped into the floral armchair across the room from my bed, then, with a self-conscious glance at me, maneuvered herself into the position my old teacher had promoted as "proper posture." Unfamiliar furniture crowded the room, from the molded wooden headboard to the dresser's little blue dollhouse. I missed my room back home, and despite what my father had promised, this didn't seem "even better" and I could still "remember what came before." At least I had a new friend already.

"Cassie." My parents insisted on using the full "Cassandra," but since they were downstairs, I might as well use the moniker I preferred, the one that hadn't proved too unwieldy for my classmates to manage.

She nodded. "I'm Gem."

"You said that already!"

She began to smile, raising her eyebrows. "It's still true."

I realized I liked her already. Not only did she dress cool; she struck me as funny, while also, somehow, profound. Had Gem done it on purpose, and anyway, why didn't people introduce themselves more than once? Even my parents seemed to know she was special, considering they hadn't made her take off her boots on the rug inside the doorway. Sure, they had ignored her, and so maybe they did not like her, but they must have respect for her. Before this, respect was something I had only seen them demand.

My mind became full of questions, not least of which was why she was talking to someone like me. I settled on the most important-seeming one: "Are you going to stay here?"

Gem smiled again, but this time, one end of her mouth turned down. "Yeah. I've been living in this room for a long time, and I'm not about to be driven out."

"That's great!" Both hands flew to my mouth, and, sure enough, my mother shouted, equally loudly, from directly below my floor: "Indoor voice, Cassandra!"

"I mean," I added, "I've always wanted a sister."

"Well, I'm not really your sister." Gem shrugged and glanced away, her soft brown hair flying in a curtain over her face. "I guess it'll be like sharing a room with a friend."

# Chapter Two

FOR THE FIRST few months, we did nothing more unusual than board games and late-night storytelling. Still, the time I spent with Gem was the most fun I'd ever had.

She reminded me of my babysitter before my parents had stopped going out, or of my parents themselves if they had forsaken shouting and the silent treatment and been at their most pleasant at all times. Like they once had, Gem stacked the Candyland deck so I would always draw Princess Lolly; as I had with my parents, I pretended not to notice. In the evenings, she taught me a different card game each week, and by the time Thursdays rolled around we could play without my needing reminders. I realized how much I had missed the time before my father's job changed, before I'd started playing with only my neighbor, Leigh, or several different imagined variations of myself.

On afternoons when I trusted my parents to stay in the rooms they were in, Gem and I searched the rest of the unfamiliar little house for monsters. In the back of my mind, I knew those sorts of creatures weren't real, not really, but I still screamed gamely when Gem grabbed my shoulders and roared, and we scampered back to our bedroom before my parents ran up the stairs to shout at me. Afterward, I spun tales about the beast we had just escaped—for Gem had jumped back into the role of non-monstrous friend by then—speaking them as they came into my head, delightfully free of logic or plot pacing. Gem seemed to like the stories, but I never failed to scare myself.

My mother had forbidden me from having sleepovers before I turned ten, but even by age eight, I had begun to chafe at her rules. They waffled bizarrely with her mood and the frequency of my father's glares. It did not take long to figure out why Gem was immune to rules: my parents did not know about her. It made sense, in a way. In my tiny world, where most of the possessions by which I defined myself were gone, Gem was really, truly mine.

I suddenly understood Leigh's moods, when she would ignore me inside her house and close the door to her giant bedroom so she could be alone with her invisible friends. My own secret friendship had been late in arriving, but now I had Gem, I figured all four of us could play together. Would we be able to see each other's companions? I wondered. Did I have control over who could see Gem, and, if I wanted to, could I keep her to myself?

As it turned out, the opportunity to test these questions never came. Now we lived in New Orleans proper, to the east of the Earhart Expressway, Leigh's home had gone from a simple trot down the road to a day-trip voyage which required two buses, a streetcar, and an apparently significant number of dollars. For the first time, I cared that my parents had no car. When several weeks went by without any sightings of children my own age, I snuck into the pantry with the phone cord navigated through the smallest possible crack in the door.

Of course, my mother recognized the situation immediately. Just after I finished dialing, she snatched the receiver with anger and a bit of resignation.

"Hi there, Brett. Is this Brett? Oh, Carol! Sorry! Well, I just found Cassandra hiding with the phone, trying to call Leigh all by her lonesome!" My mother provided a meager laugh and continued with the affected charm she piled on when forced to interact with other grownups. "Y'know, I told her she'd meet loads of kids once school started, but she just misses Leigh so much; they've always been best friends, of course. Perhaps we could have her over for a playdate—" The smile fell from her face during the long pause that followed, and her voice lowered for the few other words she had a chance to speak. "It's downtown, yes, but...we haven't seen...you know we'd watch..."

I understood the results, if not the details. There would be no party of secret friends. Even then, I think I knew: River Ridge may have been only several miles away, but it was a separate world.

IT SEEMED AMAZING at a later age, but for those first months I did not think to ask Gem about her history. I had no interest in sharing my life's story either, with my limited short-term memory. Besides, in the way of a small child with no idea what the world can hold, I saw life without imagined embellishment as hopelessly dull. Life before Gem, after all, had been mostly free of schedule or marker, and my most vivid memory involved empty threats made by a first-grade bully the previous year.

Gem offered me few clues to her origins in the early days, and most of them occurred in our first few hours of acquaintance. After she revealed that my bedroom had been hers for a while, I figured she had lived with the family who had sold my parents the house. Gem didn't have a chance to disabuse me of that notion since I never voiced it aloud.

After the awful telephone call with Leigh's family, I ran from my mother, who spit out aimless accusations in rage. "She doesn't think I can take care of kids! Thinks they're too good for us! Flaunting their money! Doubting my ability as a mother!" Inasmuch as she was talking to anyone, I knew it was more herself than me. I eased the door closed, barely catching myself before I slammed it, and spun toward Gem, predictably situated in the armchair. "What are *your* parents like?" I blurted. The question surprised even me, as I tried to avoid talking about parents, who seemed to do little but muck up young lives, but it made sense to ask. Gem's family must be wonderful, I figured, to allow her to spend all her time with a friend.

She flinched and fixed her gaze on the unkempt street out the window. At early evening, the noise from Bourbon Street had only begun to leak in our direction, and I knew I'd perform my pane-shut and curtain-draw at a slightly later hour. "They're dead."

My mind had wandered to the ambiguous threat of the outside, the morbid thrill of my nightly scampering to the curtains. "What?"

"My parents died."

"Oh, no!" I ran to her, instantly poised for a hug. "How did they die?" Later, I would shake my head at this query too; I hadn't even tested the waters with something only arguably on the uncouth side, such as "How long ago did it happen?" The daring of children can be so rude but, all results considered, undeniably useful too.

Gem did not seem fazed. "My mom died in childbirth." Seeing my face, she explained, "That means she died while I was being born." It sounded like a horrible coincidence to me. "My dad, uh...he got shot. He shot himself," she amended, meeting my eyes with steely determination. I had witnessed Gem's spunk while playing, but now it had a hard angle, defiance against façade or euphemism.

"He murdered *himself*?" I doubt I had ever heard something so perverse.

"Yeah. He was sad."

"About what?" I prompted. Gem sighed a little, but still cut her eyes at me with affection as she boosted me onto her lap.

"About me. I left...and he thought I'd be gone forever."

The conversation had become too frighteningly glum to sustain. I gave her another little hug. "I'm glad you live with us, Gem. You're my best friend."

When Gem startled me with laughter, I smiled tentatively. "You know what, Cassie? I think you'd have to be mine too."

# Chapter Three

ON MY FIRST morning of second grade, my father called me into his office as I prepared to leave for the bus. In hushed tones, he showed me a red plastic rectangle. I figured it for a toy, albeit a rather boring one, until he hit an innocuous-looking button at one end and a knife blade flew out. He showed me the way to push the blade back in, along an edge which appeared identical but was actually dull, and dropped the device into my jumper's chest pocket. I stumbled backward, not wanting it, but the weapon had already landed.

"You never know what might happen out there, Cassandra. We live in a dangerous city now, and if someone tries to hurt you, you let 'em have it, you hear me?" He pantomimed a stab, and even though the knife lay against my figure, his sudden movement scared me more. My hands went into secret fists when he spoke to me at all, let alone by myself. "Carry this every day, got it? Don't you dare let those old nuns see...but if you fail to hide this, you better not tell them you got it from me." While no longer sure what he was talking about, I knew I would do what he said, as always.

At that moment, I only cared about getting out of the house; my blood pumped violently with nerves at being near him. I waited a few moments to be sure I would not offend him by leaving before he finished with me, then sidestepped toward the door. "I don't wanna be late!" He nodded and waved me away, turning back to his computer.

I only had to walk to the end of the block, a cool distance of three houses, but it was still longer than any for which I had been unaccompanied all summer. In fact, I couldn't remember being outside in the neighborhood without one of my parents, usually my mother, alongside with a hand on me. The unnamed threats of the city had yet to show themselves, but the maddening worries of Leigh's and my parents built a mythology that was not unappealing.

When I looked at the city, I saw beauty. Small and stuffed together as our houses were, they were nonetheless ornate and colorful. The range of pastels on Dauphine alone resembled a French incarnation of *The Wizard of Oz*. River Ridge had been pretty enough and full of green foliage, but it had lacked the Technicolor wildness of New Orleans proper. No one, I imagined, would dare paint their house pink-and-white in Leigh's neighborhood. This felt like a tiny triumph. Apparently by the time one crossed the Earhart, she had also gotten rid of her colored beads, since the shiny strings swung over the hanging road signs were entirely new to me.

And then there were the lost children. Generally, they stayed farther east, along Decatur or Bourbon, or, if they wished not to be bothered at all, along the grit of the Mississippi River. I had only seen the river once by then, for a second before my parents turned toward Dauphine, but the moist, rocky terrain had fascinated me. I already knew I would voyage out alone, sometime, just to watch the water rock as I clenched the soil and let it drift through my fingers.

The only force more magnetic than the Mississippi was the runaways. One of them, I noticed with a start, sat directly across the street from me. Daringly, she situated herself in front of a house, blocked from view of the family's windows only by the sparse, dying bush which acted as the display point of their tiny yard. She resembled the girl I had seen on the day I moved in, the one with hair like matted straw and unabashed tears flowing from her face. I couldn't be sure, since she'd had her head turned downward, not to mention that vision of her had been marred by her own water. This time, the tears were absent, and her eyes were fixed on me. I turned away like the good girl I always tried to be, my father's switchblade jumping in my pocket with each step.

Around the bus stop's sign, a gaggle of unanimously cleaner girls waited in identical uniforms. They stood planted in a circle around the post, like weeds. They swiveled their heads toward me as I finished my course, hovering a safe distance away from their unapologetic stares. I wished there were a bench on which to sit, but I had already heard my parents griping about the lack of proper bus stops. Apparently, this too was the fault of the "vagrants."

"Are you newww?" One black-haired girl with a toothy grin approached me.

"Yeah. My name is Cassie." Reflexively, I glanced behind me to make sure my parents were not nearby. We fell into introductions, most girls attempting to talk over the others, a few staying quiet, already marking themselves for their Academy career with the stamp of "shy."

SCHOOL PROVED ANTICLIMACTIC. From teachers to recess, my surroundings were more or less identical to the Academy of my previous year, minus the familiar friendly faces. While being the new girl lent me a certain "flavor of the week" quality for the first portion of the school year, my new companionships paled in comparison to the vivacious tendencies of Gem.

While I was daydreaming of Gem, her boundless energy and stunningly pretty looks, Sister Mary Benita announced our third journal assignment. Generally, she had my attention at that point—Scripture was the segment for which I tended to drift, in real school in addition to Sunday school—but by the time I snapped out of my reverie, my classmates had pulled out their crayons, dotted-line paper pad, and favorite number two pencils. The subject proved easy enough to pick up, though, when I glanced at their neatly printed titles: "My Best Friend."

I knew this would be the easiest composition yet. First, I hurried to jot down the required explanatory three sentences so I could begin the centerpiece: Gem's portrait. I began with her eternally red-lipped smile, a disembodied set of smackers in the middle of the white half of the page. In several minutes, a round peach circle like a basketball appeared, topped with a complex process of brown for her long hair, with a yellow layer added to try to recreate its shine. The clothes did not necessitate a decision, considering her outfit never changed. She even appeared to sleep in her clothes, which made her all the cooler in my eyes. The tan-gray of the Boy Scout shirt, though, provided a coloration dilemma so intense I did not notice Sister Mary Benita had come to stand behind me.

"And who is this?" I straightened up in my chair, in what I knew to be the perfect posture.

"She's my best friend, Gem!" Beyond the hanging cloth of the habit, Sister's puzzled eyes fixed on the diamonds over Gem's legs. She struggled to read my huge-lettered description on the lower half of the page.

"Oh, so you share a bedroom! Is she your sister, then, or your cousin?"

"No, we're not...re-la-ted." I had always struggled with that pronunciation. "She's just my best friend. She lives with us because her parents are dead." At that last word, faces swiveled up and crayons paused on papers.

"I'm so sorry to hear that. How did she come to stay with your parents?"

"She didn't! I mean, she's been living in the house since before we were even there." At this, the teacher's eyes darkened before flickering toward me and away. She shuffled behind the student to my right, effectively closing what had existed of a conversation. While I couldn't be sure of what, the lump in my throat throughout the rest of the day informed me I had done something wrong.

I DID NOT tell Gem what had happened at school that day, even though, as usual, she asked. I had the sensation of having overstepped an invisible boundary, and part of me regretted even having brought a poor likeness of her into my drab school environment. Gem obviously knew I had a secret, as I wouldn't let myself peer into her eyes for more than an instant. After several failed attempts at starting a conversation, she turned away, her face a mask of curious hurt. This upset me, of course, but I also found it fascinating; aside from moments of self-defensive discomfort, I had never seen her sad.

That evening's phone call was much like the summer's upsetting call to Leigh. At least this time, I was only a subject rather than a participant. When my mother's voice rose, the lump in my throat returned and, setting down my Go Fish deck, I wordlessly crept down the narrow stairs and waited outside the kitchen door.

"Of course not, sir," my mother simmered, jaw clenched. "Yes, you too. Thank you." I had only a second to mourn not running downstairs earlier to catch more of the conversation. She carefully set down the receiver. Rubbing her fingertips against her palms and grinding her teeth, she let her restrained anger flare in one roared word: "*Cassandra!*"

I stepped into view, my knees already shaking.

"Why am I getting concerned calls from the headmaster?" she intoned in a deadly quiet voice. I could only shake my head. "Did you tell them we took in a vagrant?"

"A—a what?"

"A vagrant! A runaway! A homeless kid who'd been staying here before we arrived!"

"She's not a kid."

"It doesn't matter! Aren't you too old for imaginary friends? I let you talk to yourself; I figured you were just creative, but if you don't know the difference between fantasy and reality, you have a serious mental problem, young lady!" She began to pace, staring straight ahead instead of at me. I gave myself permission to cry. "Do you have any idea how bad you've made us look? Your father and I are good, upstanding Christians! We would never enable those whores and drug addicts." Halting, my mother turned back to my cowering figure in the doorway and lowered her voice again. "Goddamn it, you've humiliated us, Cassandra." As often when she became like this, my name was a curse. "I can't imagine what we did to deserve this." Turning away, she began to sniffle. "Go to your room, brat, and don't come down until you know the difference between true and make believe—and are ready to apologize for what you did to us."

I slumped against my closed bedroom door. Gem's eyebrows were raised. "What the hell is going on out there?"

"Please don't swear," I whispered. She rolled her eyes, and though I had never explained my squeamishness to any friend before, I added, "It reminds me of them."

"Oh." Gem moved toward me with a gentle hug, and I folded myself into her. She felt like a combination of my old babysitter, a participant in the embraces at the ends of Leigh's animated movies, and the way I imagined God, if such a thing existed.

"I wrote about you at school." She sighed and extricated herself from my arms. "I'm sorry!" I cried. "I didn't know—"

"Shhh." Gem brushed back my hair, and I studied her face, which did not appear too upset. I could have stared at her forever, though she glanced at me no more than any object in the room, or than my parents, when we passed them by. "You didn't do anything wrong. People just don't...understand me. What I am."

Fear twisted my stomach. What if Mother had been more accurate than she knew? "Are you a kid?"

"What? Not really. I'm fifteen."

With a deep breath, I asked the question that both thrilled and terrified me: "Are you one of the 'lost children?'"

Gem sighed and stretched out on the armchair, her long legs dangling from the left arm. "Depends, I guess. What does that phrase mean to you?"

"Um..." I tried to plan my words while recalling what information I had actually managed to assemble. "They're teenagers who ran away from their families, ran away to New Orleans, and they don't have homes."

"Then, no. I'm not. I did run away once, but not from my family. Besides, I grew up in this city. I didn't have a chance to make it into a utopia." Her final word lost me, but I understood enough. Gem was a runaway, but not cruel enough to leave her dad. Despite her conclusion that she was not a lost child, I started to think of her as a softer, more enchanting variation on the category: my spunky, beautiful lost girl.

"Do other people have friends like you?"

Gem twisted her face, pensive. "I don't think so. If they do, you'll probably never know it. There's only one of me, at least." This impressed me; what made me so special? I remembered Leigh, speaking to empty space in her room, with a thrill of superiority. *So she* doesn't *have the coolest house.*

"Why can't they see you?" I asked finally.

Gem's lips lifted into the sly half-smile I already knew well. "The question is, why can you? No one else has been able to see me for years." I found myself staring again, wanting to ask more but not knowing what might upset her. That day alone, I had proved my inadequacy at predicting the sore points of adults, and Gem was basically one herself, from what I understood about teenagers. Then my father's heavy shoes approached the doorstep, my mother's furious whispers grew nearer, and my insides tingled with knowing dread. When he burst through my door, I barely had time to notice his puffy hand flying through Gem's torso as if it were air.

BY THE TIME my tears dried that night, I may not have comprehended most of the grownup world any more firmly, but I understood some things were too special to share. So long as I had Gem's maternal hand on the small of my back, stroking the beginnings of a bruise in sympathy, I had all the validation I needed.

# Chapter Four

I WOULD NEVER say I enjoyed the Academy. Still, given the scenes in my home, I learned to disengage enough to show up for one hundred and eighty days per year with a minimum of psychological damage. Generally, I refrained from getting too personal with my classmates—or, higher powers forbid, the sisters. Certainly I never attracted the attention of the headmaster for the remainder of my elementary years.

By fourth grade, I had gained a reputation for utilizing the library a lot, but that was as malicious as rumors got. I had learned my lesson about putting my honest, vulnerable self forward. On a regular basis, I reminded myself that failing to join a clique could hardly be considered a *failure* at all. The supposed BFFs I observed either made each other cry with words or held amateur fistfights in the fields which ended with parents being called.

The categories usually divided themselves between the girls and boys, respectively; all the more reason to stay out of the tangle. I wasn't willing to mimic my mother in calculated shouts, and on the occasions girls did fight physically, their punishments proved harsher. Some of the stricter sisters lectured brawling girls on womanly behavior, a talk I couldn't have received looking sincere. In fourth grade, two of my female classmates were even expelled after a fight. From what I could tell, theirs had been no worse than the fistfights between boys. I wanted no trouble from fickle friends, not to mention the authorities within the Academy's gates or Dauphine Street's homes.

*School does not matter.* By my tenth birthday, I repeated these words in my head daily, like a mantra, but I had trouble believing them myself. Academics may matter some day, and I put work toward them to prevent the possibility of this bigger future falling away. The social snow globe of our elementary campus, though, seemed aimless, full of unhappy kids and adults eager to inflict their own discontent onto one another. Sometimes I wished for their company as I turned my pages in the library chairs at recess, but then I would remind myself I had a cool, older best friend at home with whom to talk about the world and distract from these petty dramas. What resentment or loneliness I did feel, I learned to stuff inside me.

"You're smart, you know," Gem concluded the first time I explained my approach to school. It wasn't the first time I had been described this way; the refrain on my report cards tended to be a variation on *Very bright, very shy!* While I would not have called myself *shy*, I understood how the mistake might be made, and I had to acknowledge that by schooling definitions, *bright* was a fair descriptor. "I never had the greatest perspective, myself. At your age, school drama seemed like everything, and it only got worse as I got older." She leaned forward in the armchair, a pointed finger inches from my nose in a half-joking admonishment. "Don't let junior high change you, okay? Promise?"

"I promise. It won't be that different, anyway, since junior high is just on the other side of the campus. All the same people will be there."

Gem cringed. "You'd be surprised. When I turned thirteen, everything changed. Every*one* changed." I turned my head toward her on my pillow. We had established early on that Gem had not attended my same Academy, had been to public school, but while it must have also been in New Orleans, I did not know where she had gone. Now my peers and I were aware of the competing elementaries' test scores; the sisters often pulled me aside to talk about them, specifically. I realized it might mean something to find out more. "What was the *name* of your school, Gem?"

She started slightly; I rarely asked her about her life, though increasingly curious. "Wells."

I repeated the name in my mind. "I've never heard of it."

"Naturally. It got torn down a long time ago."

"Oh." While I had accepted early on that Gem never seemed to grow, or dirty her never-changed clothes, I found myself wondering: *How long has she been fifteen?*

WHEN CLASS LET out for lunch the next day, I power-walked—running would attract attention, and possibly even discipline—to the library, eating the sandwich I'd prepared with one hand. Lately, I had come to wonder if packing a lunch was worthwhile at all, since it acted as a daily obstacle to my reading.

After the library door had closed behind me, I passed by my favorite section, Fantasy, eyes averted with purpose. While fourth, fifth and sixth graders did not have a limit on how many books they could check out, I tried to keep only one at a time, to read at home, while I spent my breaks working through other, unchecked stories in-house. Research, as a rule, gathered dust in the corner, remaining untouched by all students unless there were reports to be done. *Oh well.* One lunch period of less-than-stimulating reading would be a small price to pay if I turned up anything fruitful.

Twenty minutes later, I had to reevaluate. With lunchtime half over, I was bored of New Orleans' yellowed newspapers and had seen no mention of Wells Elementary. Worse still, I had not read a page of the tome about dragons I had been working on all week. One more paper, I decided, but after I glanced at the front page, the thought melted away.

Though black-and-white, the photo of the fire almost felt hot. The flames raged over deteriorating structures, well on their way to becoming more piles of debris, still smoldering with specks of deadly light amongst ashes. I could not remember seeing something, even a work of art, which managed to be both so gorgeous and so menacing. Minutes must have passed before I even saw the headline: *Local school burns. Police suspect arson.* The scene, then, had been as horrific as it looked. I read on: *This Saturday, the Seventh Ward's Wells Elementary School—*

Spots rushed through my vision, so I put my head down on the paper, breathing hard against its stale scent, until I stopped feeling dizzy. Then, I read on, and continued to the following day's paper, and the days' after that, riveted, no longer daring to skip a single edition.

I OFTEN SAT with other girls on the school bus, though we did not speak much. That afternoon, I intentionally sat alone. I had barely heard a word of our final lessons yet had come no closer to figuring out this gigantic puzzle.

The story in and of itself had proved salacious enough to fascinate the press for weeks: a teenaged arsonist, a possible suicide attempt, hundreds of children displaced, myriad parents struggling to transfer their kids' schooling mid-year. My nails had dug into my palm, painfully but, somehow, necessarily, until I reached the point at which the arsonist's name had finally been released: Daisy Soren. She was a girl from Texas who had run away from a boarding school in Baton Rouge the previous year. She had acted alone, and seemingly without motive. Much of the press focused, bizarrely, on her diverse ancestry. Daisy had stayed secretive even when convicted of her crimes as an adult; she had covered her face in defiance, hiding from reporters.

If the criminal had been Gem, I may have had to become a runaway myself, but it hurt to even think about it. I knew Gem would never do a thing like that, but then, she had told me her school had been "torn down." Why would she say something so misleading? *Did* she have some dark secrets?

Plus, while I knew it reflected poorly on my priorities, I could not forget for a second that Wells had burned down in 1970. Though barely twenty years, it seemed like ages ago, and I did not like the idea that Gem had been around so long. In any case, Gem probably was what I would consider *old*.

I WAITED UNTIL the evening. Conveniently, it was Back to School Night, and for once, our parents' turn to be bored by the sisters and docents. For only the third time in my life that I could recall, my parents deemed me acceptable to leave at home without a sitter. I'm certain the question of money made their decision easier. When they boarded the city bus on the corner, I paced myself up the stairs and into our bedroom.

As usual, Gem sprawled in her favorite chair, reading the sci-fi novel I currently had checked out. I ran through the questions in my mind, and when I spoke, all the words I could say filled my body until something burst out. It was not the most logical question, but I had not had a choice.

"Who's Daisy Soren?"

Gem dropped the book. I winced as it flopped on my hardwood floor, spine open and face down, but Gem did not seem to notice. All went quiet for a second; we were locked in a stare. Finally, she spoke low and with restrained wrath: "What the hell have you been doing?"

"I... Don't swear, Gem," I whispered.

"'Don't swear?'" Gem bolted upright onto her feet. "How about, don't pry into my history, Cassie? Cassandra?"

"I'm sorry!" I blurted. "I just, I wanted to know about Wells—"

"Wells?" Gem repeated blankly. She let out a hard breath and dropped her eyes, contemplative. "The fire. You read about the fire." I stayed against the wall, silent, until her face rose and her own fire returned to her eyes. "Is there a reason you didn't just ask me?"

"I don't know. Why didn't you tell me it burned down?"

"Oh, no." Gem shook her head wildly. "Don't start acting like I did something wrong. Maybe I don't like talking about certain parts of my life, huh? If you're really curious, maybe I'll share if you deign to *ask*. Did you ever think how I'd feel learning you've been snooping around for information when I'm right here—literally, right here!—all the time?" Her eyes became shiny, and for a strange second I wondered. If she cried on Mother's carpet, would Mother be able to see the wetness?

Knowing I'd hurt Gem, let alone made her angry, was more than I could take. I turned and ran before the tears could fall. Obviously, Gem had seen me cry on a number of occasions, but it seemed infinitely more shameful now it had been caused by her. Before, she had been my refuge, the closest to a dependable force my life had. As I scurried down the stairs, I told myself this would never happen again; I would not do anything to hurt Gem.

Once in the yard, I closed my eyes with hopeful words in my head and realized I was praying, though to what, I couldn't imagine. The God of Scripture seemed a terrifying entity. While Jesus softened the concept, I could not fathom heaven, let alone the other idea most of the sisters and docents seemed to preach: that everything happened for a reason. *If they could only read my mind,* I thought with a bitter chuckle. *Their star student is a heretic!*

When I reached up to touch my cheek, I realized I had stopped crying. Still, I didn't want to go inside and face my friend's anger. Besides, I realized, excitement bubbling in my stomach, my parents would not be home for hours.

I crept down the road, the noises drifting from Bourbon already loud. The night air settled around me, thick and hot as soup. The silence was heavy too, punctuated only by the chirrups of unseen bugs. I studied houses like mine, sherbet-hued and compact and crumbling at the edges, as well as buildings abandoned entirely. Tree branches and tangles of ivy burst through old roofs, strangling the empty houses from the inside. Even the graffiti was beautiful: painstaking colorful images of animals and solemnly staring women. I stopped walking only when two rats sprinted across the narrow street before me.

Until I reached the French Quarter, there were no other humans. Just like I had always heard, when they appeared, they all seemed to be headed toward the jazz and lights of Bourbon Street. I sidestepped onto a different road before too many jolly adults could study me. Royal was lined with ornate mansions and glass-covered shops, but now night had fallen, it was as dark and quiet as my block had been.

I paused at a corner, below the canopy created by several balconies layered on top of one another, next to a closed storefront on the ground floor. Running my fingers along the vine-like white posts, I had the feeling, for the first time, that this city was present especially for people like me, to give us comfort when we felt alone. Even the street corners were beautiful, and though I indeed stood in solitude, I imagined where I stood as a likely place for the lost children to go and think at night. I sat upon the sidewalk, wishing I could stay and watch the world from there.

And then I saw, with the same sense of rightness, something the world had to show me.

Two women stumbled down a side street, directly toward me. They were fairly young; I would have guessed in their twenties, but I had a notoriously bad track record for the guessing of ages. Both wore pants and sleeveless shirts, and I found myself studying their faces and chests again to be sure they were indeed women, because in their laughing, unsteady gait, they held hands.

I stayed silent and still, as unobtrusive as I knew how to make myself.

"I'm so glad you were free tonight," the smaller one with pale skin and hair announced breathlessly. "I've never had the nerve to go out by myself."

"Out drinking in general, you mean, or to the dyke bars?" The bigger woman had dark skin and hair hanging all the way down her back; still, she had been the one I had first found harder to identify gender-wise, maybe since her clothes were loose enough to obscure her figure. Hearing their voices, I no longer had any doubt. They stopped below a streetlight on the opposite corner and turned to each other. In the light, they were both beautiful.

"Either, really." The first woman wrapped her arms around the other's shoulders in a hug, leaving just enough space between them to maintain eye contact. Their noses were close together.

"So, see anything you like in there?" the other murmured, moving her hands around the woman's tiny waist.

"You know I did," she replied, in a whisper I could barely hear, and their lips came together.

I clapped a hand over my mouth and cursed myself for a tiny noise, but I doubt anything I could have done would have disturbed the couple by then. They kissed hungrily, mouths widening and grips tightening as their hands caressed each other's backs and hair. I had never seen anyone, let alone two females, show affection like this. Though I overheard classmates talking about their "crushes" on occasion, I had always wondered whether the type of passionate love in movies truly existed. Then again, I had never seen a film adult enough to include making out of this caliber. I suppose I had become a bit of a cynic even by then.

Love shone on their faces, clear as day, along with something else I could not quite identify. As for their genders, I had never known about women being in love with each other, but it made all the sense in the world. When I had imagined meeting a boy appealing enough to fall in love with before, it had seemed far-fetched if not impossible, but if there were a woman...

When their palms began to explore each other's bottoms, I sprinted back to the house. This simply seemed like too much for me to handle.

"I'M SORRY," I whispered as I slipped into bed, clothes still on.

"I am too," replied Gem, who, had I not experienced the earlier scene with her, would have seemed utterly calm. "I shouldn't have yelled. I just dealt with some hard stuff in my life, and you caught me off guard." I pondered the implications of her past tense, and as if on cue, she added, "You really are welcome to ask questions. Do you have any right now?"

Of course I did. I buried my head in the mattress and breathed, "How did you die?"

Gem paused. "You didn't look it up already?" All at once, my suspicions were confirmed. I knew of no other supernatural creatures that went from human to inhuman. While she didn't look like a white sheet or Jiminy Cricket's Ghost of Christmas Past, I had a ghost for a best friend.

"No. I didn't think to. And I wasn't sure, you know...if you *had* died."

"Oh, I'm dead all right," she said wryly. "Does it bother you?"

Images of skeletons shaking their bones jumped into my mind, but I said, "No. You're still you." Gem smiled. "Are there ghosts everywhere?" I added, just to put my mental morbidity at bay.

"No. Or if there are, most of us can't see each other. I don't know where all the other dead people go," she added, "so don't start asking me big questions about the afterlife." I nodded. It may seem strange, but the topic had not occurred to me. "So, my death. Well, I ran away from school to come back here, and I got into some trouble on the streets. To make a long story short—which, uh," she hurried, probably sensing the extent of my curiosity, "I think is the best idea right now, a lot of dangerous people just weren't too happy with me. Some of them figured out where I lived, where this house was. On my first night back here, they got in." I shuddered despite myself. "I could hold my own in a fight, make no mistake," Gem added, "but they were armed."

"Armed?"

"They had weapons." We both fell silent.

Finally, I ventured, "I'm sorry."

"Don't be. You weren't there. And besides...it happened." I reached out and put a hand on her shoulder, and we gave each other small smiles before she retreated to her chair for the night.

Before I fell asleep, I remembered my feelings at seeing the photographed fire again: awe and horror. In retrospect, it had been appropriate for that day, which had been more terrible and wonderful than I could have imagined.

# Chapter Five

ON MY FIRST morning of junior high, I rushed around the house, nervous, while a bemused Gem observed from the kitchen table. I knew she remembered my vow not to change as well as I recalled my conviction in making it, but with a playful cut of the eyes, I dared her to say something.

Over the summer, I had begun to reconsider my philosophy against trying to make friends in school and keeping to myself as much as possible. Our class hours would now be extended, and I would be stuck on campus longer still if I took on extracurriculars, which both intrigued me and, I had been told, were necessary if one was serious about college. Shyness might no longer be my best option. I wasn't changing, I told myself; I had simply come to care more about making a good impression. For many teachers and classmates, it would be my *first* impression.

This detail had not become apparent until my father had taken me to explore the campus the week before. Mother had picked up an extra day's worth of work, leaving Father stone-faced in annoyance over the "pointless journey" and "wasted bus fare." I, however, found a number of problems on our brief walk through my scheduled classrooms. For two grades, the junior high campus was huge. Somehow, it seemed even huger than it had when I had been eight; then again, it tended to be gated closed during the school year. It had the air of an exclusive club...or maybe a prison. *This is a different world,* I thought. *We're expected to become new people while we're here. People who can't be mixed with the kids of "k" through "six."*

"Hey, Dad?" I hated calling him that, but I knew he preferred it. Father had often rebuked me for calling him "Father" at church, saying people would think I was afraid of him.

"Yes, Cassandra."

"Why is this campus bigger than the primary's?"

He frowned and swiveled his head back and forth as if he had not noticed. Perhaps he hadn't, having not spent as much time on the younger grades' campus as I had. I wondered if I had stumped him. "Classes are smaller, I think, since they're more based on individual interests. And there's the matter of new students, of course."

"New students? We never have that many."

"I meant, from the other elementary schools. The public-school punks whose parents think they're smart enough to go here instead." I stopped walking. Public school kids? Transfers? Why hadn't they told me this earlier?

"How many do you think there will be?" I asked, carefully casual.

"How would I know? I think your mom said it was fifty-fifty or thereabouts last year."

My stomach turned a somersault. I had enrolled in a new type of school, on a campus I barely knew, when I'd never even seen half of the people who would be there before? Not only half, I corrected myself; I certainly didn't know most of the eighth graders, even the ones who had been at the Academy. From what I had heard about kids from the public schools, they were not adept at leaving people who did not blend into one of several crowds alone. I had no idea what to do to avoid bullying.

That morning, I still felt lost before even leaving the house, but I had crafted a vague plan around finding other smart kids. I would need allies, after all, and this seemed the wisest way to go about finding a flexible group. Even so, I couldn't shake the feeling: this year would be unlike any school experience I had already had.

"I just want to get through this whole school thing as painlessly as possible," I griped to Gem as I pulled my newly clean, and crumpled, uniform from the dryer. I held its warmth against my neck with a sigh before sauntering over to my waiting iron.

"That's a good approach to have to middle school, hon," Gem replied, tilting her head back over the chair and catching my eyes from upside-down. "Anything else just sets the hopers up for heartache." She paused, thinking. "Should I go ahead and tell you that? Or should I let you believe it'll be great and hope the expectations make it so?"

"Not an issue." I rolled my eyes mid-iron. "I'm not the type of person who expects school to be great, especially at a religious place like the Academy, where we sit packed in tiny rooms, snoring at God-talk." I smiled, despite the unappealing qualities of the subject. For the last few months, I had come to enjoy my conversations with Gem more than ever before. I understood all the words she used now, as if I were her equal. Better still, I found our attitudes more and more compatible with each week.

I picked up my pleated skirt and held it to my legs. It seemed shorter than it had been in June, which was possible, considering I had grown several inches over the last year. If our minds were primed to become sex-crazed, as last year's Human Growth and Development course seemed to suggest, I wondered why junior high upgraded the girls from long skirts to ones that didn't reach our knees. Wouldn't people find it distracting? I already feared *I* would.

I reached for the elastic of my red-and-white striped pajama pants and paused, glancing at Gem while I felt the beginnings of a shyness totally new to me. As unobtrusively as I could manage, I buttoned my skirt around my waist before pulling my bottoms off underneath; she didn't seem to notice. Gem preoccupied herself with eating the last of Mother's toaster pastries, and while I knew I would more than likely get yelled at for the offense, I did not try to stop her. Gem's eating fascinated me, since she had no human body with which to digest or metabolize it. Sometimes when I found it hard to sleep, I mentally debated theories about exactly when the mashed-up food disappeared into thin air, not to mention where it went. Besides, she was undeniably cute, and as childlike as ever, with fruity goo and cream cheese smeared across her lips.

When my ivory-colored blouse had been smoothed to my satisfaction, I glanced at her again and felt silly. It was just Gem, after all. I pulled my top off over my head, not bothering to unbutton since it was so much bigger than my torso. Instinctively, I reached for my blouse before glancing down at my chest and sighing. Holding the bunched-up flannel over my breasts, I sprinted back to the bedroom for my new bra. Even that little bit of running made my chest hurt.

As it turned out, the process Human Growth and Development had dubbed *becoming a woman* was a hassle. I went back and forth on whether I should look forward to bleeding for the first time; periods seemed to hold a certain mystique, while my breasts had so far done nothing but, quite literally, get in the way. I had worn my biggest T-shirts all summer, but my breasts had seemed to view this as a personal challenge, and one at which they had surely succeeded.

Before the trip to the department store with Mother, I had seen Father whispering to her fiercely with glances at my torso; I went back and forth on which part of the day had been more humiliating. I once flipped through a teen magazine that said to stay close to your skin color so the acquisition won't show through your shirt, so I'd nixed classic white garments. I had relented for the pink bra, simple and elegant, pale as the Wandering Chopsticks roses in Jackson Square. If I needed to trouble myself with a bra, it would be this one. It was a few shades lighter than my skin, if not more. Still, if there were any justice in the realm of underwear, the shade would be close enough. Even if it had not fit properly, I might have insisted upon it.

I bounded back down the stairs, putting on a casual face, despite this being only the second time I had worn the pretty garment. Gem glanced up and did a double take, and any illusions of glamour fell away from me. I envied her lack of necessity to ever change her clothes. "It's awful, I know," I groaned, secretly wishing she would contradict me. "Mother says I have to wear it."

"Cute bra, but yeah, you probably should." Gem shrugged, any discomfort gone, unless I had imagined it in the first place. "I mean, if you don't want to show through your shirt."

"Of course I don't!" I threw a couch cushion at her as I picked up the blouse again. "I don't want the headmaster to stare."

She stopped licking her lips of leftover pastry crumbs and swiveled to face me. "What?"

"They say he stares at girls." I finished buttoning as I spoke. "They say he gets creepy when they're, you know, showing a lot." Grabbing the fabric of my skirt, I playfully lifted it a bit in demonstration.

Gem jumped out of the chair and stood directly in front of me. We were nearly the same height. "That's not funny."

My hands fell to my sides. "I..." I began, but I had no idea what to say.

"I'm serious." Gem's eyebrows knitted together, her voice hard.

"I don't know if it's true!" I tried hastily. "It's just what the kids say. They're probably making stuff up out of sheer boredom!" I forced a chuckle; Gem's face stayed wooden.

"Still. Sexual predators aren't a joke. Trust me, they're out there, a lot of them, in fact, and when they hurt people, it's *totally* not funny." She broke her gaze and stepped back a bit. "You still carry your dad's knife, right?"

"Yeah, always, unless I'm here."

"That's good." Gem put an arm around me and smiled slightly, but without joy. "You don't let anyone hurt you, okay? Promise?"

"I promise." I returned her half-hug, glad the moment was over. Then I glanced at my watch, and, with a frantic grin, pulled away from her for another run to the bedroom. I threw the blade in my pocket, rechecked the contents of my backpack, and after another hug, I went out and away.

LIKE MY NEWLY obtrusive breasts, junior high struck me as more chaotic than exciting once I had actually passed through the gates. The scant minutes between each session were an absurdly inadequate length of time to get to our next classroom. The mostly silent walk with my father had not helped, and I found myself so busy worrying over my schedule I hardly noticed the new faces until lunchtime, except to note I seemed to be surrounded by strangers. The eighth graders and new kids seemed to swell to a majority well over fifty percent.

And the eighth grade's girls were, simply put, women. I was afraid to study them until lunchtime, when gawking apparently became an accepted mode of action amongst those of us in only the seventh grade. I ate my sandwich huddled outside my previous class, in the company of four other nameless girls my age who were as silent as I was. The eighth graders, who more closely resembled Gem than me, were more clustered together than Academy Primary students had ever been, and they passed us in wave after wave. All together, they formed an ocean of lipstick, open buttons and *legs*. Good lord, their legs went on forever, skirts covering barely a fraction of their lower halves. They didn't seem inhibited as they jumped up, and scurried toward one another. *That one*, I thought, *looks like an older version of—*

No. I went still inside. Could it be? I only saw her from behind until she spun backward to greet another scurrier, and then there could be no doubt. One of the glamorous girls I had assumed to be older than me was none other than my old friend, Leigh. *We must not have had any classes together today,* I mused, half-shocked, *at least not yet.* I should have recognized her, not just anywhere, but immediately. Leigh remained more petite than most, resulting in a more compact body than her gorgeous friends', and her face still resembled its six-year-old form. I studied her thick makeup for several seconds before I realized she was staring me in the face. Our eyes met, and Leigh turned and continued on her way, flanked on both sides by young women in identical chokers.

I told myself she had probably not recognized me, but somehow, I could not believe it. I wanted to cry but focused on my breathing, returning to the second-most riveting people-watching session of my young life. Near my post at the south wing, the hall monitor nabbed one young lady for a dress code violation in the form of sheer rather than opaque tights, and another daredevil who had actually attempted to get away with fishnets. Unlike Gem's brown legwear with its complex pattern, these were the classic, blocky black version of college students visiting our city on break, or jacketed exotic dancers passing past Dauphine on their way to or from work. I wound up so distracted I never ended up having to decide whether to head for the library or not, because the bell rang before I had even finished my sandwich.

IN THE DAY'S final two courses, I was both relieved and disappointed to note Leigh's continued absence. I noticed a few of the seventh-grade girls, about half of whom I remembered from my primary days, had developed as well. As I had predicted, the blouses proved inadequate at hiding who had, and had not, finished their flat-chested days. Several times, I reminded myself to avert my eyes; anyone paying specific attention to me would notice where my gaze tended to be drawn.

*But* is *anyone watching me?* I wondered. A redheaded boy turned back in his seat to glance at me several times, and I averted my eyes, annoyed. Like most of the boys in this grade, he was tall enough to have snuck over from the other campus; otherwise, they did not appear older at all. Apparently, boys did not go through a transformation in which they became magically appealing before eighth grade, either. My elective, Arts and Crafts, turned out to have several kids from the class ahead of us, including the starer, whom I never would have guessed was older.

While Mathematics finished, I pondered the problem of gym. The next week, when we began to change for the session, should I duck into the bathroom? No, I admitted grudgingly; that would only call attention to me and attract a label like "prude." I had better just throw on and remove my clothes hurriedly, eyes on no one's body but my own, and pretend the other girls couldn't see me either.

"So, do you think you're going to go?" a faceless voice prompted. I looked to my left to see Jill, a nice and studious Academy girl with whom I had partnered on several projects in the last few years.

"Sorry—go where?"

Jill giggled and smiled with her eyes at me, as if we were sharing a secret. "He's pretty dull, huh?" she whispered, motioning subtly to the teacher. "I meant, are you going to the Back to School Dance?" I noticed the flyer in her hand then, bright orange in some facsimile of autumn festivity.

"Oh. I don't know yet...are you?"

"I think so." The happy anxiety in her eyes hinted it was not a question to *think* about at all. "You should come! You can hang out with me." I smiled and nodded, thinking, *why not?* Making friends might be easier than I had assumed.

WITH A WEEK of junior high under my school-mandated patent leather belt, I opened my closet. While I didn't have many clothes, the options overwhelmed me. Since I had always attended institutions with uniforms, I had no experience dressing for my peers. During summer or the weekends, I switched between favorite pairs of shorts and pants and colored T-shirts, mostly without design. While I could appreciate the outfits of passing ladies, I had never been inclined to care what cloth I put on my own body. With a sigh, I mentally acknowledged I probably would have to *learn* how to care.

Gem startled me at the doorway. She glanced at my face and the open closet and seemed to grasp the situation immediately. "Just wear what makes you feel like you."

"Uh, Gem? I have no idea what that means. Who else would I feel like?"

She stepped forward and began to flip through the hanging articles as if paging through a heavy book. "Cassie, it may not seem like it now, but when you ask things like that, you're pretty damn ahead of the game." I thought of protesting her use of the d-word, but I had grown less sensitive to swearing since my schoolmates had picked it up in the last few years. Besides, it did not come off as offensive unless she was angry. When I stopped to think of the word itself, I knew I had no objection to its supposed blasphemy.

"Well, we can't all have your gift for expression," I returned, mostly joking but a little bitter.

Gem whirled around. "Huh?"

I gestured toward her permanent ensemble: badge-laden Boy Scout shirt, short green skirt, brown fishnets and tan boots. "I'm going to go ahead and guess your other outfits were just as spunky and daring." She smiled a bit, and I knew I had come to know her well. "So, we've been living together for five years. Why don't *you* tell me what's 'me?'"

"Because I can't. No one can. It has to come from in here." She put her palm forward as if to lay it on my heart, then pointed at it instead. "Besides," she faltered, drifting back to her chair, "I don't even know who you're dressing for."

Maybe clothing did have its own exclusive language. "Explain, please."

She grinned up at me, and I could not remember having this sensation of towering over her before. "Is there someone you're hoping to dance with? Some...boy?"

"No!" While I had heard gossip over the past few days over who might dance with whom, it stunned me that Gem would think I wanted to participate in those rituals. The idea of dancing with a boy, which presumably entailed putting our hands on each other, sounded alien and unpleasant.

"No boy in particular, or no boys at all?" *What is this about?* I wondered. Gem's eyes had gone narrow and serious, bordering on interrogative.

"At all. I don't, uh..." My heart began hammering, though I could not tell exactly why.

"Yeah?"

*It's okay,* I told myself. *Gem's your best friend, and she's seen a lot. She won't think it's weird.* "I don't think I really like boys," I confessed. "I mean, I like some of them as people, I think, but you know—"

"You don't want a boyfriend?" I kept my nerves at bay, but Gem leaned forward; something was definitely on her mind.

I shook my head truthfully. "I don't think I ever will."

"That's okay, you know," Gem said gently.

"Is it? I mean, I don't know why it wouldn't be, but sometimes people act like all girls do. Have you... I mean..." My voice fell to a whisper. "Did you ever know girls like me?"

"In any case, yes," Gem began, eyes locked on my face, "but what type of girl are you talking about? Are you not attracted to anyone, or...?" A long silence stretched between us. "Do you think you might want a *girl*friend?"

My face heated up. "Yes. That sounds a lot better."

Gem's face broke out into a grin. "That's awesome!"

"It is?"

"Yes!" She leapt up and gave me a quick hug, laughing. "Oh my God, you just *came out* to me! I take it I'm the first?"

"First I've told? Duh." As if I had someone else to tell. "What's so awesome about it?"

She began to calm down. "Well, first of all, it's awesome you know this about yourself so early. A lot of people don't. What's really awesome, though, is women. And, don't worry: there are plenty of other gay girls out there."

"'Gay?' Isn't that just men?"

"No, it's for anyone same gender-loving. And yes," Gem added, though I had only ventured to ask in my mind, "I am, or was, I guess, gay too."

I sat on the edge of the bed and wondered if I should skip the dance after all so Gem and I could spend the evening talking about this. My secret had never weighed me down like a burden, but having shared it, I felt a lot lighter. *No*, I decided; *I don't want to upset Jill.* Still, we took full advantage of the thirty minutes before I would need to catch the bus.

It was lucky my parents were out, because I had countless questions, and I doubt I could have remembered to keep my voice down. When I finally bothered to check the clock, I hopped up with a start, threw on jeans with the first shirt I spotted, and ran out of the door within a minute.

*It's funny,* I thought, jogging onto the bus seconds before it sped away. *I really do feel like "me" right now.*

BY THE TIME we had finished inching past Canal Street, my optimism had become clouded. *Should I really be proud I'm different?* I wondered. Gem said so, but she also said people would oppose me for no real reason if I liked a girl. In the springtime especially, when the tourists flooded in, people made fun of men with boyfriends, or men who might want boyfriends. I made a habit of paying no attention during church, and sometimes even snuck to the chapel library for the duration of the class my parents walked me to, but I could remember the teacher denouncing gay men at least once. If anything had been said about lesbians, either by him or my peers, I had missed it.

Here, then, was another reason to socialize: so I could identify those who would and would not support me. I had a feeling my parents would fall into the latter category, considering how invested they were in good Christian appearances. For now, I knew I had better keep my feelings from them as usual, lest they exile me from the home.

When my eyes drifted across the aisle, I shuddered despite myself. Speak of the devil. A sandy-haired homeless girl stared at me with watery eyes from directly to the right. I thought I had seen this particular lost child before, but I ignored her for the duration of the ride and then hurried off the bus. The last time I had been close to a homeless person, he had screamed nonsense words at me when I had tried to give him a dollar.

Our gym had been transformed into another planet, under a sky of reflective multicolor streamers. Rather pretty, in a kitschy way. "Cassie!" Jill cried, waving her hand from the opposite edge of the room. I did not remember telling her I preferred the nickname over Cassandra, but it pleased me to hear it from her. I approached to find her standing with two other girls from the primary, each with a transparent cup of red punch in hand. Jill made introductions, and while I can no longer remember either of the others' names, I recall the tall one who played sports speaking first.

"I can't wait to dance with some guys!" She scanned the room with a nervous smile. "I know we can ask them too, but I don't think I could do it. Too scary."

"You should," said the other. "I'm going to when a slow song comes on, at least if I don't get asked first." The conversation fractured into merits of several boys whose names I did not recognize, and finally Jill nudged me.

"Who would you dance with, Cassandra?" Maybe I looked as distant as I felt, since she'd reverted to my formal name. "I mean, if it could be anyone."

"I don't think I would. I mean...I don't really like any of these guys."

"I know what you mean," the second girl sighed. "It doesn't have to mean anything, though. It's just a dance." Seconds later, I felt a hand on my shoulder. It was the orange-haired eighth grader from Arts and Crafts.

"Hey, Cassandra. Wanna dance?"

We stood in silence for several seconds. "I don't know your name," I said finally, and wanted to kick myself when the giggles erupted behind me.

"It's Mackey. So, how about it?" He already sounded impatient. *It's just a dance,* I thought, and nodded slightly before following him onto the floor. He laid his hands on my hips and, after glancing at the other couples for guidance, I stretched my fingertips up onto his shoulders. *There is no way I'm pretending to like guys for the rest of my life,* I decided. As the song progressed, Mackey's hands drifted lower, and a nauseous lump formed in my throat. I told myself he probably didn't notice, and I would only embarrass him if I showed my discomfort.

Before the song finished, he leaned forward and whispered, "I found something cool the other day. Do you wanna go see?"

"Yeah!" I replied, relieved. Maybe this was the purpose of our dancing, and his staring, after all. In a rush, I crafted a backstory in my head: Mackey wanted to be friends with me, but girls and boys being friends was taboo, so he acted like he wanted to do the socially acceptable thing, dancing, when really it was just an excuse to start talking. With any luck, we'd have more in common than I thought.

Confusingly, he led me into the corridor for the restrooms, then opened an unlabeled side door. "Come see!" he insisted, stepping inside. I ducked around the open door, and before I could blink, he had pulled it shut and pushed me against the wall.

My eyes darted around; we were in a small, square storage room, empty except for a machine in the corner that read SHOP-VAC. "Welcome to my secret hideout," murmured Mackey, leaning in close. I tried to scoot away, still not quite feeling the danger, but he pushed against both my shoulders with his strong hands. My heart jumped into my throat as I dodged his kiss. "Hey, relax," he hissed, annoyed.

I breathed harder, wondering if I should beg him to let me go, if there were any chance he would take pity on me. "No," I whispered when he trailed his pointer finger over my neckline.

"Shh, it's okay." He pushed harder. "C'mon, girl, don't you like me?"

"No!" I exclaimed, as loudly as possible, but I knew no one outside would hear me over the music. *If I could free my hands*, I thought, but by now he had both my arms pinned over my head. My mind raced for another tactic.

Mackey saw my mouth moving and leaned in for another try at a kiss.

He came just close enough for the glob of spit, when I released it, to hit him in the eye.

My shout for help had been nothing compared to his unearthly shriek. The switchblade landed with a clatter as both Mackey's hands flew to his face, and I snatched it up and threw open the door. A large group of my classmates stood, immobile, their own eyes locked on us in confusion and shock. Like a scene from a cartoon, even the music had stopped. When several kids rushed into the pantry and emerged with Mackey, still clutching his eye as they comforted him, I snapped out of my daze. I pivoted on my heel and ran.

"Fuckin' dyke!" Mackey called after me.

Throughout the week, I had mused over reputations, over labels: the outlines of personae my classmates either adopted or ran from in attempts to define themselves. I had not opted to participate in their strange charade but, as I fled their searing gazes, I knew my role had already been chosen for me.

BY THE TIME I slammed the front door, my feet were steady and my eyes were dry. When I told Gem the story, though, the tears poured out of a terror deep inside me. We did not turn any lights on, but by the time I finished, I could tell she wept too.

"You're amazing," she whispered after I explained how I had gotten away. "I'm so proud of you. Now he might even think of you before he tries to hurt anyone else." I had not thought of this, and it gave me a sense of pride.

"I was just so scared."

"I know. God, I know…" Gem began sobbing, and it scared me all over again. "God, Cassie, you have no idea. I couldn't bear it if anything happened to you. If you were assaulted, I would die." I suppose this should have seemed ironic, but I knew what she meant. I could imagine the sensation of an inner death, a dying of which you feel every pinprick because you're cursed to stay alive the entire time.

I lay down and sank into my pillows. "Gem?" The answer scared me, but she had told me I could ask her anything. "When you say…you know…?"

She leaned over and hugged me fiercely. "If I get into that, I'll probably have to tell my whole story. Are you sure you want to hear it? You probably have years to learn all my secrets. I'm afraid to burden you with them at your age."

I wanted to know everything about her. "I'm old enough. Tell me. Please."

Gem retreated to the armchair, took a deep breath and bestowed on me what is still the most incredible story I have ever heard.

# Chapter Six

ONE AFTERNOON IN 1965, a precocious young preteen walked behind her classroom's trailer at Wells Elementary to find two unfamiliar teenagers hidden from the rest of the campus. They were a girl and a boy, and they were eating unidentifiable bits from a mint box. Gem had been elected class representative of the sixth grade, and she was on an emotional high as she skipped out of class an hour early, teacher sanctified, to attend her first meeting. Today, she could not be disturbed by anything, let alone a couple of red-eyed older kids in a place where they should not be. She wondered if they were involved in the construction on the main building.

Apparently, it never even occurred to Gem that the couple constituted a threat. Like me, she had been too willing to believe the best of people, even though her life at home was, also like mine, lacking in joy.

She sat to talk with them. Gem had been fascinated by teenagers since she had seen two women holding hands as a toddler, and though this appeared to be a heterosexual couple, Gem found herself curious about their lives. Perhaps she had much to look forward to, and when the boy offered her a mint, she did not hesitate.

Immediately, the world went funny. The concrete below her bottom began to waver, and the lightly blowing branches above Gem seemed to take on new, frightening forms. The real horror occurred some time later, when the pair began to kiss Gem and put their hands under her clothes. The details were hazy in her mind, or at least she chose to say so, and I didn't want to hear about what had happened anyway. Mainly, she remembered them laughing, as if the whole thing were a lark. Later, as she still lay overcome with dizziness, the two left, with a warning to Gem: she had better be back at the same time the following week, *or else.*

When Gem felt well enough to walk, she took herself home, forgoing the bus for which her father had given her money to have a few minutes alone. After shutting the front door of our house on Dauphine, she went straight to bed, failing to do her homework for the first time in her life.

EXACTLY A WEEK later, she woke up trembling. Gem considered going to a teacher or the principal for help but nixed the idea. The playground, after all, had an unwritten rule against revealing the indiscretions of others to the yard duty. Besides, Gem knew what had happened was wrong and even dirty. She had never heard of rape but had read a little about sex, and it definitely was not something children were meant to be doing. Since her body had been the scene of the crime, she worried sharing would implicate her too. Plus, she had taken their strange mint. *Candy from strangers.* Surely everyone would think she was as stupid as she did.

It hurt me to hear Gem had thought this way. For the first and only time as she told the story, I interrupted, to whisper, "It wasn't your fault at all, Gem."

Before returning to the story, she squeezed my hand, and, to my relief, responded with, "I know."

In the end, she crept behind the portable as she had been told to, while the class representatives' meeting went on elsewhere. Gem was deathly afraid of what the pair would do to her if she did not obey them, considering what they had done already. She thought maybe if she begged them not to hurt her, they would take pity.

It did not work out that way. When Gem refused to swallow another "mint," and showed clear resistance to their intentions, they pinned her down and held her nose closed until she opened her mouth, then dropped the item down her throat. Later, as they took advantage of her state, other faces rushed toward them. Gem assumed these other people were hallucinations too, until the couple stood up and fled.

Gem's teacher, who had released his students for the day then been alerted that something was going on behind the building, stood over her with the yard duty in tow. Roughly, the men pulled Gem, barely conscious and only in her underwear, to the main office, where she gathered her wits to find the principal, the superintendent, and her ashen-faced father around her, all both shocked and interrogative.

When Gem revealed this had happened before, everyone stepped farther away from her. Within minutes, the school officials in the room had convinced Gem's father she should continue her education at a special girls' boarding school in Baton Rouge, equipped to deal with "troubled" students, even the sort who had been caught performing "unnatural acts." The collaboration of the superintendent seemed a special blow, as Gem had always found her beautiful and dreamed of being on the auditorium stage with her, receiving one of her infamously rare academic awards.

GEM DESCRIBED THE following month as "hell," in no uncertain terms, and I could believe it. Her father would barely acknowledge her, and when she finally shouted at him to please talk, he took to avoiding the house altogether. She began spending her days in the library. At first, she kept her eyes averted from the section with local yearbooks, but she gave in and pored through the former year's high schools'. Within an hour, Gem recognized both of her assailants. She felt vindicated, somehow. She would not dare go to the police considering what had already happened, but the monsters who haunted her mind were real; they had names. Years later, she would hear they had both been sent to prison for drug possession, but at that moment, at the age of eleven, her comforts were meager.

As her day of departure grew closer, Gem began to panic. She could not understand how she could possibly be sent away, when, all her life, she had been a rather well-behaved kid. The worst act she could remember committing was stealing small items from stores, and even then, she had only done it after forgetting to bring money.

As a final act of defiance, Gem refused to pack. On the morning of her departure, though, she woke to an alarm she had not set to find two full suitcases sitting on her bedroom floor. Her train ticket sat on top of the larger one. More to the point, Gem awoke to the realization that life in this house would be unbearable to continue. Besides, she could hardly have made herself face her scandalized schoolmates if she *had* been welcome to rejoin Wells. Even if she didn't belong at the reform institution, Gem figured, it would have to be better.

BOARDING SCHOOL, TO hear Gem tell it, turned out to be both stifling and boring, a strange combination of half-hearted education and juvenile prison. On the one hand, most of her classmates were either unmotivated academically or had given up on the system, and for the first time ever, Gem managed to be the top student in her grade rather than remaining a runner-up. She continued to stay dutifully ahead on her homework, though a nagging voice in her head asked why she bothered. After all, her father had been recommended to keep her enrolled through high school, and Gem doubted many universities would consider her if they recognized her school's name.

On the other hand, however, lay everything else. The work itself rarely proved mentally engaging, for one. The guards and so-called Hall Mothers kept an exhaustive surveillance on each student. They chaperoned each study session, meeting of more than two girls, and trip to the drugstore for hygienic necessities. Each pupil could count on her night of sleep being interrupted by hourly flashlight checks; surprise occurred when, in the morning, she could not remember having been woken up at all. When class schedules necessitated a walk to another building, let alone when a student attempted a visit with an acquaintance, a guard patted the entering girls down to make sure they had not been handed something dangerous by someone outside.

Talk of escape seemed common, but in Gem's first few years within the high fences, no one attempted it. Despite their supposed mark as juvenile delinquents, the most trouble the students ever seemed to get into was occasional fistfights or being caught with cigarettes, liquor, or pot. Gem knew those things happened at "regular" schools as well.

Family visits and departures for vacation were strictly forbidden in the year-round school, although the students could telephone home once a week. Gem never did. The one time her father called, to make sure she had arrived and, essentially, been taken into custody, she refused to speak to him, leaving the Hall Mother to icily reassure him of the school's commitment to changing the course of her life. He sent her letters roughly once a month, each free of questions and full of statements about how he hoped Gem was doing well. It annoyed her that he pretended to care at all, especially when some of her hallmates teased her, calling her "Daddy's little girl." She saw the letters as a self-indulgent easing of guilt, an ease her father did not deserve.

IN NINTH GRADE, Gem met Daze.

From her first day inside the walls, Daze stirred up trouble. The staff members soon referred to her, with varying degrees of affection, as "Hellcat." Amongst the girls, an unwritten rule existed against asking one another about what had landed them there; local wisdom assumed it barely mattered. Daze, however, made no bones about the fact that during a drunken beating by her mother, she had hit the woman over the head with the family Bible and given her a concussion.

Daze's big mistake, she often said, had been calling an ambulance, thus enabling the police to get involved. They had uncovered and pored through Daze's journal, which included several violent fantasies against her mother, because, she said, "I'd have to be lobotomized not to wish she were dead!" Like Gem's father, Daze's mother sent her postcards aggressively concerned with appearances and apparently amnesiac to the reason Daze had been sent away.

Daze also did not appear concerned with standards, particularly when they involved social norms. She washed her dark blonde hair and few clothes less frequently than most of the other girls, earning constant gripes from her roommate. The often-greasy mess on top of her head was never tied up; she tucked her hair under a black knit beanie or left it hanging free and unapologetic. Daze sometimes attempted to skip class by sleeping in, prompting a team of guards to storm into her room before walking in late, in her pajamas. Most shocking of all, she spent the entirety of her allotted drugstore allowance on additions to her collection of cheap red lipsticks, ignoring tampons and napkins. She let herself bleed onto her sheets and a pair of black pants every month instead. Daze forwent Kleenex too, even though it was readily available in most classrooms, and wiped her nose on her sleeves. The few times someone commented on the crispy bits of fabric, Daze would, without warning, shout something along the lines of, "I make do with what I've got! Worry about your own body."

Gem fell in love with her right away.

FOR THE FIRST few months of Gem's relationship with Daze, they rarely had a moment alone. Privacy was precious for any friendship, but at least no one on the campus seemed to raise an eyebrow at same-sex relationships, though there were only a few at any given time. Gem found their nonchalance refreshing. In her young life before boarding school, queerness in men and women alike had been ridiculed, except on Mardi Gras, when kissing between strangers seemed to be *de rigueur* or even a party trick.

I, on the other hand, had been methodically taken to my grandparents' in Metairie for the duration of Mardi Gras each year. I tingled in jealousy for Gem, who had often snuck out to marvel at grownups acting uncivilized.

They held long talks and make out sessions within their respective dorm rooms, but a Hall Mother would burst in "for a check" at least once an hour, with no telling exactly when each check would occur. Sometimes, the other occupant of the bedroom would barge in, and it came to the point where both Daze and Gem could have sworn their respective roommates were interfering on purpose, for a laugh. While Gem had been fairly popular since her first year, she had never been assigned a room with someone with whom she could bond.

Then, one night, Daze interrupted Gem's hall's dinner time with elation in her eyes. Even the routine patting down she experienced at the door could not curb her excitement. Gem finished eating and stepped outside to meet her girlfriend, wading through copious amounts of good-natured ribbing from her hallmates. Once the two had gotten inside her ground floor bedroom, Daze opened her closet, identical to those in each room, all designed for safety. Without a word, she went to a corner covered with crumpled clothes and pushed the pile aside, uncovering a sheet of cardboard which Daze then removed to reveal...a hole.

Gem never figured out what Daze had used to create it, and felt a frisson mixed with fear at the reckless damage to the room. Still, her heart nearly overflowed when Daze took her hand, led her down to several feet of space below the floor, and lay with her on a thin blanket spread out over the dirt.

If Gem and Daze could not make love within school walls, they would do it below them.

BY THE SUMMER, and final session of ninth grade, the couple remained deeply in love but had grown used to each other. They no longer spent most of their time underground. Though the staff had seemed troubled by Daze's rebelliousness at first, Daze had charmed most of them by the time the weather grew hot and sticky. Gem understood; after all, she and Daze knew everything about each other, and what was not to love?

When the two went on the same drugstore run one evening, Gem realized she had not revealed everything after all. When she pocketed a ChapStick, Daze poked her in the ribs. "The hell are you doing?" Daze whispered, staying out of the auditory range of the two guards only a few yards away.

"Oh." Gem started. She had come to shoplift so frequently since beginning boarding school she rarely even considered it anymore. "I...take things sometimes." The closer guard walked toward them; speaking in lowered tones, especially outside of school walls, was always suspicious. "I'll tell you later."

Back in Gem's bedroom, though, she found her activity harder to explain than she had anticipated. Daze's confrontation made her uncomfortable. "It's just a way of saving money, I guess. I know I can get away with it, so why shouldn't I? It'd be a waste not to." She found herself wringing her hands, more nervous than she thought she had cause to be.

"You could get caught, you know." Daze's tone was flat. "And then you'd be sent to juvie, real juvie, not like here."

"They wouldn't bother. Most the students are here for drugs, which is way more serious than shoplifting. Besides, I usually try and make it look like an accident even if I was caught. Just give me a chance to show you."

Soon after Daze complied, the two finagled their way into another outing, despite having little money left for the month. Daze stayed silent so as not to draw attention as Gem demonstrated her tricks: holding a product for a while, using it, and putting it in her bag or pocket as if that were where it had come from; seeming to struggle with carrying everything, shoving an item in her purse to help the matter, and appearing to forget about it. When the time came to go, Gem walked through the door as if without a care. Even though there appeared to be an employee always stationed near the doorway to keep watch, sure enough, Gem remained untroubled.

As they lay together before the hall curfew, Daze confessed, "I don't know about this. It's not like big companies need our money, but it's still a risk for you." It surprised Gem, as this reaction didn't gel with what she had come to know of Daze's Hellcat persona. Did the devil-may-care attitude only apply to the actions of Daze herself? Her worries were sweet, Gem conceded, but kind of condescending.

Needless to say, she didn't stop shoplifting. In a dull week, it gave Gem a feeling of having accomplished something, however small. When she saw it as a typical part of her girlfriend's life, Daze's reaction started to change, and she asked questions like, "Have you ever tried to take something big?"

By the end of the summer, the conversation had segued into something more expansive: plans to flee the school. If Gem could hone her skills to a sharper degree, maybe the two would not have to worry as much about procuring essentials once they were on their own. The drugstore run would be the time to flee too, since although it might be expected, it would be much safer than attempting to wreak havoc on enemy turf, surrounded by guards with their jobs to protect.

Unlike the other people who waxed poetic about escape, Gem was serious about not spending three more years locked away like a convict. Her goal was not to create another entertaining, cinematic plan; it was to craft, and carry out, a plan that could work.

THE BIG DAY arrived in the form of a calm twilight in October.

The couple stepped into the van of the teacher fulfilling night duty avoiding each other's eyes, adopting an air of careless nonchalance. Gem had one of Daze's many red lipsticks in tow along with her secret stash of purloined matches and the dollars she had managed to save. Daze carried nothing but cash in her pockets and had donned her tall-heeled boots. She had been careful not to put them on until just before stepping out of her building, and then they both had been careful to arrive at the van at the stroke of seven, before the driver had had time to drive around for and pick up the guards.

A guard would not have let those boots go unexamined. She would have known the deception of which they were capable.

If one or more other students ran up to tag along, the plan would immediately be aborted. Somehow, though, Gem knew none would, and had a feeling Daze had the same sensation. Tonight was the night.

GEM NEVER KNEW exactly how Daze got the knife. From what she had gathered, it involved complex connection with the outside, and she had wondered aloud if it wasn't a waste to sneak something in just to try to get back out with it. Daze seemed to know what she was doing, though, despite most of the plan having been formulated by Gem. Playing a facsimile of themselves on the drive over was agonizing, but the two had never managed to stay quiet for a twenty-minute period before and were not about to raise suspicion then. After puttering around inside the drugstore for a minute, Daze announced a need to visit the ladies' room. Gem fought to keep her gaze straightforward, though her dramatic side itched for eye contact.

As usual, one guard accompanied Daze to the bathroom, which lay beyond a complex series of dank rooms typically only meant to be seen by employees. The other guard and the driver kept an eye on Gem, who had to step up the subtlety on her shoplifting tactics. She wondered if she needed to buy something at all to prove necessity for the trip, but the adults were used to girls tagging along for no other reason than to breathe a little off-campus air. All the same, Gem pretended to be frustrated at the sight of an empty rack amongst the makeup. She never wore makeup, but others often assumed she did thanks to her clear skin. Gem knew the guards' lives were filled with more student minutiae than they could have wanted, but she did not flatter herself into thinking they cared about her cosmetic habits.

Several minutes later, there was a scream.

The remaining guard and the teacher rushed back toward the bathroom, leaving Gem unguarded. She exited, as unobtrusively as possible, out the automatic doors while the few customers and employees froze and began, instinctively, to panic. Predictably, a small drugstore with a locked-up pharmacy had no hired guards of its own for a still Sunday evening.

Once outside, Gem sprinted toward the back end of the building, stopping only to hand the lipstick and instructions to the omnipresent homeless man along the west side. She didn't like having to depend on another party, but the cash she flashed from her sweater pocket would have to be incentive enough. As soon as he uncapped the item and headed for the front door, she dropped the cash on the jacket he had left to mark his spot and soldiered on. Gem reached the newly shattered bathroom window just as Daze hopped to the ground, not needing her catch after all. If only they could keep heading away from the front entrance, away from the van...but a long metal fence divided the property from a neighbor's backyard. They turned back and ran toward growing shouts. The man they had enlisted appeared to relish his role as an ambiguous threat, coming at innocent caretakers with horror movie-esque brick red bleeding from his face and neck, his casting as the id's image of dementia.

Gem soared as she never had before, flying on adrenaline, which made her scrape the ground with her face even harder when a strong hand grabbed her around the middle. The teacher, whose name she still didn't know, had his face locked into a wild leer as he tackled her and then held her against the van with his entire body. She turned back, blood still coursing. Her homeless ally growled at their guard against the side wall, blocking the guard's access to the girls with his body. He appeared to be having entirely too much fun. As time seemed to slow down for Gem, she worried for him, as they would certainly all be arrested now she had been caught.

It also was strange to see only one guard outside. Was the other still in the bathroom, and if so, why? Defeated, Gem's eyes flicked to Daze, who had stopped short at the edge of the lot. Silently, Gem sent her the message to go on, but instead, Daze removed the knife from her heel, preparing to charge back. In an instant, Gem had a burst of inspiration and stamina and jerked her hand back into her pocket. A second later, the teacher stood agog as Gem held a lit match over the gas pipe. "You wouldn't dare," he hissed, turning white. She dropped the match in.

It did not create the fiery explosion she had half-hoped for, but a flame flared up immediately, rapid in growth. He dropped her entirely to run, screaming in inhuman terror as both the guard and her ally spotted the situation and fled. The air became a chorus of screams, mostly unfamiliar, which shook Gem out of her stupor and carried her to a waiting, and clearly impressed, Daze.

Despite the situation and her love's flushed face, the first thing Gem noticed was the thin line of blood along the knife. "She thought I was bluffing, kept coming at me," Daze panted. "I had to cut her on the knee." Their gaze broke, and without daring to glance back, both sprinted away.

They did not stop running until, despite adrenaline, they both had pains in their sides, and even then, the couple knew they needed to get farther away. Daze stepped forward on the sidewalk and lifted her thumb as if she had been doing it for years, and soon, a young man not much older than them pulled over. Gem could still hear the sirens in the distance as they stepped inside his battered sports car. No sooner had they slid back into the road than Daze lifted her knife back up. She calmly examined it in the light of the streetlamps, but the driver noticed it immediately. The threat was implicit.

When the man nervously asked where to go, the girls were silent. Despite having left in an unfair form of disgrace, Gem craved the moody beauty of the Crescent City, but she also knew the school would have people searching for her there within a week. Finally, Daze directed him several hours south, to an area neither knew well and would not be expected to approach. Daze herself was from the west of Texas and seemed to hold no sentimentality for her hometown. After choosing an arbitrary drop spot, Daze made veiled threats against contacting cops in a sweet voice, and the two chose an alley in which to spend the night.

As they situated themselves against the wall, Gem was happy not to be in New Orleans, for the first time in years. There may have been a sense of camaraderie between the young runaways, but the homeless were just too ubiquitous there. For that night, she did not want to be disturbed. Gem had to lean halfway against the dumpster when Daze wrapped her arms around her, but she didn't mind, even when a sticky film adhered to her hair and tank top.

Gem tried to sleep, but the shocks of the day wouldn't leave her. She had known they would genuinely try to escape; moreover, she had known she *had* to try to escape, because Gem could not take any more life without change. Honestly, though, maybe she had not expected them to succeed in getting away. She would have been less surprised if she and Daze had now been in separate makeshift cells in the police station, gazing at each other over their handcuffs.

THE FOLLOWING MORNING, they ate like queens at the local diner and plotted their next move. The meal cost, all things considered, a good amount of money, but Gem figured they had earned it. Besides, her first task would be to procure more food and supplies, so there would be no need for a splurge for the following days. Daze stayed at "home"—their dumpster—while Gem scouted around the nearest strip mall, making note of the shops without any appearance of serious security. When she returned hours later with a new backpack full of food and tissue, she found a semicircle of characters in their twenties around her girlfriend, talking and laughing with her. Always the charmer, Daze had made friends.

GEM DESCRIBED THE following weeks to me with obvious reluctance. It amazed me that, after all she had been through up to that point, she could be so affected by what happened next. I suppose this is what authentic heartbreak can do.

WITHIN DAYS, HER girlfriend started dealing marijuana and acid. While she understood the decision from a practical point of view, Gem was troubled at the ease with which Daze stepped into her role as dealer. Daze's Hellcat instincts were uncanny regarding which locations to stake out and when, exactly, to step out of the shadows. She would have been more disturbed if Daze were a user, but though Daze admitted to having experimented in the past, she assured everyone involved she would not jeopardize her valuable stash. Besides, Daze often reminded her,

Gem had smoked pot before herself, and it had led to a set of matches that had saved their lives.

Gem felt increasingly useless. Her own brand of criminality was only necessary in bursts, and she knew her sense of being unequal might have heightened her irritability. Still, when their first fight occurred, Gem held to the conviction of being right.

"What the hell are you doing?" Gem demanded one afternoon, as she headed home with a bag full of new acquisitions. By chance, she had spotted Daze loitering outside the local Krystal, a popular fast food chain with a sign imploring its customers to *Get the Happy Krystal Habit*! "I thought you were trying to sell today." But Gem was already angry because she knew exactly what was happening.

"This is a big after-school spot."

"Yeah, I'm aware. And I repeat: what are you *doing*? You can't deal to kids."

"Gemmy, they're in high school, or junior high at the least. Most of them are as old as us."

"I know, but..." She could not think up a logical support, though; Gem could barely think of anything but the faces of her two teenage assailants. She considered the obvious argument about children being too young to make such a decision, but Daze would know she didn't actually believe it. Gem had lost the debate already. Then again, did Daze not understand why this scenario disturbed her? After all, she knew what had happened to Gem as a child.

Tensions increased, and Gem found herself transferring her discomfort into worries over Daze being caught. She knew her concerns were out of proportion, especially considering her own dubious relationship with the law, but Daze seemed recklessly confident. The two fell into a pattern of fighting about Daze's methods at least once every few days. Before their first month of living free had ended, Gem discovered how easy it could be to wrongly think she knew everything about somebody. After a particularly bitter and fruitless fight, Daze shouted, "For God's sake, I've been doing this a long time! I know what I'm doing!" As soon as she said it, they both froze.

"What?"

Daze knew she had trapped herself. "I dealt at school, a little. I mean, it was just something to do." Soon, the torrid story came out, and, not for the first time in her life, Gem marveled at her own naïveté. She had assumed, with the harsh security within school walls, that drugs never made more than a quick appearance. *Of course they did*, she scolded herself now. *Where there's a will...* and then there was the way Daze seemed to hold sway over some of the staff members. How clueless she had been.

"Is there a reason you never told me?" Gem began to boil over, not just at Daze, but the long, unfair course of her life, in which she always seemed to be cast as the fool.

"A girl's got to have her secrets." That did it.

"No! She *doesn't*, Daze! When you love someone, when you want her to trust you, you tell her if you're a fucking drug dealer!" The fight raged on without borders, full of words Gem could not and would not care to remember a day later. Finally, an idea occurred to Gem, one so senseless and out of character it felt right. Pretending to be contrite, at least for the night, Gem lay next to Daze in the alley, on stolen blankets, and waited for her to fall asleep.

At a late hour, Gem reached under the blanket in the space between them and pulled out both of their backpacks. After opening Daze's, she gasped. Daze had kept more than her past from her, apparently, because Gem had never seen so much money in one place.

She transferred the contents of Daze's bag to her own, pushed the empty pack back underneath the blanket, and set off.

THIS TIME, OTHERS' judgments be damned, Gem knew she wanted to go home to New Orleans. It wasn't difficult to get lost in the city, let alone to avoid a limited social figure like her father. Typically, the drive between Baton Rouge and New Orleans stayed within one afternoon, but then there had been the night of hitchhiking, of driving far south with Daze's self-assured smile and the glint of her knife.

In a gas station, Gem took hold of a free map of Louisiana. She did her best to estimate the time it would take to walk. Minutes later, the attendant asked her to leave, despite the fact she had been wearing her latest outfit less than a week and would not have guessed she looked like a ragamuffin. It was just as well. When Daze reported what had happened to her supplier, Bo, more than a few citizens on the street would likely have an eye on her.

Hitchhiking could potentially get her home in a day, but unlike Daze, she carried no weapon. Besides, Gem had tired of depending on other people. She just wanted to walk and walk, sweating her first love out of her system.

Gem had never been athletic and frequently had to stop. Then again, she figured, she was on her own time, for the first time in her life. During the days, she walked parallel to major highways with her eyes wide open, seeing more of the world than she ever had even while limited to the expanse of southern Louisiana. She stopped only to buy water, and only when she became dizzy and too dehydrated even to sweat. At night, she found a place that seemed relatively safe, again, inside or next to a dumpster, which held the bonus of often being full of wasted food. Several times, men approached her or tried to intimidate her, but she ignored them and kept walking with as much determination as she could muster. A week later, a familiar blue sign read *Welcome to New Orleans*, but it was hardly necessary; Gem felt the city's approach below her skin.

She walked unhurriedly, taking everything in until her heart hurt with the impact of what she'd been missing: the street signs high up, beads endlessly wound around their wires; the traffic backed up for miles by the brick-red streetcars; the ornate French décor like icing spread unevenly throughout the neighborhoods; the lack of pretension worn like a badge by the citizens of the Ninth Ward as they walked home. She too, finally, was home.

Though Gem had learned to deride Café du Monde for its tourist implications years before, she stopped along Decatur on impulse to partake of the pastries. As she ate, she stared out at the artists selling their gorgeous original wares along Jackson Square, waiting diligently each day for the rare customer with the right combination of appreciation and funds. Without warning, her throat began to hurt and tears built up. Finding she still recalled the Café's prices, she threw money on the small table and ran the remaining blocks.

There it was, the house on Dauphine Street. Gem sank to her knees and cried in front of it for some time, not caring who saw her, before entering. The spare key remained in its original hiding place. Gem stripped off her Boy Scout shirt, skirt, and tights, all of which were now filthy from the days of walking through dust and mud and gathering sweat, and ran them through the washer and dryer. If the consistency of her father could be counted upon, and she would bet it could, he would not be home until late in the evening. She would figure out her next move then.

Gem had not planned to put her traveling outfit back on, but she opened her closet to find clothes that had not fit her in years. Even if they had, they no longer represented her tastes or who she actually was. When dusk began to settle, she redressed herself and, giving up the idea of going back to the street immediately, settled in for just one night's worth of sleep in her old bed.

As soon as unconsciousness settled over her, her window shattered.

Bolting upright, Gem found herself staring down the barrel of a gun, behind which sat the contorted, merciless face of Bo. "Did you think you could run away?" Gem did not have time to form an answer before her vision exploded and her face collapsed in on herself. She stepped out of her body.

And that was how, one week before Christmas in 1969, Gem came to die at the age of fifteen. After all she had been through in the previous four years, she took her last breath at home, in her childhood bed.

"I GUESS DAZE still remembered my address from my father's letters. But I don't...I don't think she really thought about what would happen when Bo found me." We both were quiet for a while.

"And your father?" I whispered.

"He found me the next day. He didn't take it well, of course. I never thought someone so stoic could fall apart like that. I stood in the middle of the room like *this*, and I could see myself on the bed. I didn't even really understand I was dead yet, just dreaming or hallucinating or something. My father obviously couldn't see me, even though I yelled at him that I was fine. He walked through me, finally, to call the police. Right through me." Gem sat back down, eyes on her lap, and it took her another minute to continue. "I accepted I had died the next day. It was silly, what did it. I held my breath and realized I could hold it forever and still feel fine. I didn't need to breathe.

"It took me longer to figure out why my dad hid the gun in his room. It seemed so stupid, because if anyone found it, of course they'd think *he'd* killed me. Turned out, he'd already given up. He died in this room too, by the same weapon I had. If his coworkers hadn't heard about *my* death and come to check on him, he might have rotted here."

I shivered. "Were you there?"

Gem finally began to cry. "Of course. I'd already figured out I couldn't leave the house. It was worse than anything when I was alive. I screamed at him, tried to hold his arms back, everything. I even told him I forgave him, though I don't know if I really did. Pretty soon, it was over." I reached to take Gem's hand again, and we didn't speak any more.

THE NEXT MORNING, I drifted awake but kept my eyes shut. Unlike some mornings, I immediately remembered everything that had happened, and felt frozen to my sheet. The idea of another day overwhelmed me. My mind flashed back to Mackey with his hand just above my chest and my ineffectual shouting, then I pictured attackers waiting for Gem in this very room, and a terrible chill went through me. To calm myself, I pictured the enviable sweetness of the early days of Gem and Daze. *Gem and Daze...*

*Daze?* My eyes popped open.

Surprisingly, it was still early enough to be dark outside. Gem stood by the window with her eyes unfocused, and she started when I spoke. "Was it her, Gem?"

"What?"

I had the sense, for some reason, she already suspected what I would ask. "Daze. Was she Daisy Soren?"

Gem sighed. "I thought it might take you longer to put that together. Yes. It was her."

"But why..." I still vividly remembered the photograph of Wells Elementary in flames.

"I guess she meant to avenge me, somehow."

My eyes welled up. Apparently, I hadn't cried myself out the night before. If her school still had trailers and was under construction, it might have been easy to start a fire that spread and spread like, well... "What happened to her?"

Gem sat back down but did not face me. "She intended to go down with the school, but the firefighters got there too soon. So," she hurried, "she finished the job in prison. Found something to hang with, from what I've read."

I shuddered, wanting to take Gem into my arms but not knowing if she would let me. "I'm sorry."

Smiling sadly, Gem again replied, "You weren't there."

# Chapter Seven

JUST AS I had heard, junior high continued to be rather horrible. My reputation as the school dyke, the one who started to make out with a boy and then physically hurt him, proved unshakable. Still, I had allies who were friendly enough to spend most lunch periods with, and I suspected many others did not believe Mackey's version of the story either. Part of me wondered if I had acted irresponsibly by not telling other people what he had tried to do, but more than anything, I wanted to forget the awful night had occurred altogether. If I believed Gem, I had done good just by fighting back, but I did not feel equipped to be the Academy poster child for victims of sexual misconduct.

As for Arts and Crafts, I managed to switch into French with a minimum of hassle since it was still so early in the year. I did not want Mackey to have the satisfaction of scaring me off, but I couldn't coexist with his leering eyes and giant hands five days a week. Every time I saw him, I replayed the attack in my mind, and even though I knew I had gotten away, it made my heart race and my palms sweat. Instead, I met Asha, a sweet and quiet girl with whom I came to spend much of my in-school downtime. Jill continued to be a friend to me as well, though I sometimes had the feeling she joined others in making fun of me behind my back. I hardly blamed her if she did; I knew I didn't fit in with my classmates. Most days, my own self-esteem was intact, and Gem told me that was all that mattered in the end.

Ah, Gem. On the worst days, when crowds of boys would make a show out of edging away from me in mock terror, Gem was the only reason I managed to maintain my perspective. Her presence reminded me: what my classmates did couldn't tear me apart.

Gem also served as physical proof, if not the living and breathing kind, that it was okay to be attracted to other girls. Despite the many hardships Gem had experienced in her short life, she had never let being gay act as an obstacle to her. I knew Daze's gender had not affected the messy way things had turned out between them. Gem still spoke of her with compassion, and often iterated that, had she survived, she surely would have moved on to have other loves.

Impressively, Gem claimed to have few regrets aside from her impulsive stealing of cash. What she and Daze had shared had been special and authentic, even if the other girl had not turned out to be as stable as she had hoped.

At these times, my best friend seemed very wise, but this may have been inevitable after decades to think about all she had experienced. The unusual part was that, at the age of thirteen, I could be privy to her valuable insights. It made children my own age seem all the sillier and allowed me a sense of not unpleasant superiority.

JUST LIKE ANY other hard time, seventh grade concluded. I bought myself a yearbook, uncertain of why, and had a great many classmates I barely knew sign in a rainbow of colors. Both the activity and the actual notes felt, in the end, disingenuous.

"I just feel ridiculous for even participating in these rituals," I told Gem after the final day had let out, perusing the signatures I had gone to the trouble to acquire. "The only ones that even seem honest sound like this: *Thanks for helping me in math.* Oh, here, this one's even better: *I had fun in math with you!* Am I wrong, or is there a pattern here, a very depressing pattern?"

Gem laughed harder the more I spoke. "You know, it's amazing. Some things never do change. If it makes you feel better, every student, and I don't just mean at the Academy, has a few of those, even if they specifically set out to avoid them."

"Thanks." I rolled my eyes and added, "But it doesn't, by the way." Even the entries to and from honest-to-goodness friends, meaning Asha or Jill, were awkward to ask for and performative to write. I was disappointed their brief paragraphs hadn't held more emotion, but I wouldn't tell Gem that. Instead, I waded into another potentially mortifying topic. "People were talking about what they wrote for their crushes, or vice versa. Girls discussed it, which didn't surprise me, but the boys did too. It was weird."

Gem rolled her eyes. "I'm not surprised. The two are not as different as most of the mainstream wants us to believe."

"No. I mean, I feel so different from *all* of them. This sort of yearbook crush code never would have occurred to me. I don't have a crush or anything," I added hastily, "but even if I did, this doesn't feel intuitive." I spoke the truth. While there were a few girls I found exciting to look at, I had not met anyone who seemed worthy of daydreams. I had not connected with any of them. In truth, though, I had barely tried. Even aside from my shy tendencies, I could not imagine any of them living up to the lively, witty, wise magnetism of Gem.

I glanced at her, thinking she had fallen strangely silent, and re-angled the conversation. "You know, one person opened the front pages after they were pretty full and said, 'You popular girl!' just like that, really loudly. I think I blushed. I couldn't even tell if she was making fun of me."

"Could be, but I doubt it. Everyone's probably too busy trying to figure out how popular *they* are or aren't. I'd be surprised if this girl's sitting around pondering your misleading yearbook pages. But even if she did mean it ironically, what do you care? Who is this girl to you? Oh, wait; I'm sorry: Did you two *have fun in math*?"

I threw a pillow at her, and she returned fire. We were still laughing when Father pounded on the door and told me to keep it down.


ON THE FIRST day of summer, I grabbed my uniform, headed for the bathroom, and got halfway into the outfit before I realized I had been freed for the next few months. I debated whether to shimmy back into my pajamas to grab new clothes, but the finicky process seemed like too much for a relaxing season. Besides, when I listened, I could tell both my parents were out of the house already, and since Gem had not been in my room when I woke up, she was probably downstairs using the computer. As I changed, her footsteps began, and I hurried into my underwear, shirt, and shorts.

It troubled me to admit, but in the privacy of my own head, I could not deny I had developed a bit of discomfort with my best friend. Gem never annoyed me or anything, but her presence distracted me when I should have been thinking about homework. Then, of course, I felt weird about changing. This was typical, I reminded myself, being that Gem was in my same age group...in body, anyway.

I knew I had gained a significant amount of weight over the past year. I cared more about what Gem might think of my body than any of the girls in gym, and gym had been uncomfortable enough. Once summer school started, I decided, I would work in my father's study whenever he went out. Gem would understand. I found myself wishing I had my own room to retreat to, even though I still would have spent most of my time with her.

*MARDI GRAS RAGED around me.* How did I get here? *I wondered, knowing my parents said the "scene" was no place for a "kid." Soon, I forgot all logical discrepancies, as is so often the way. I took to staring at the floats, decked out with papier mâché, blinking lights, extravagant masks, and women of every shape and background. Some displays constituted pseudo-historical recreations, some declarations of pride for myriad different groups, some no concept more organized than pure joy.*

*I stood on Canal Street, marveling at the way it had been transformed; even the streetcars were nowhere to be found. Strangers crowded me from all sides, but they did not feel like a threat. A smile grew on my face, the goofy sort that, on others, would probably make me assume they were on drugs.*

*"One of a kind, isn't it?" Gem stood at my elbow in a simple purple dress. Her presence did not surprise me,*

*but I forgot the parade at the sight of her. I had no desire to take in anyone or anything else. I followed her pointed finger, though, when she told me to "Look," expecting a particularly impressive costume. Instead, there were two old women kissing with abandon, and I knew, somehow, they had been together since they were teenagers and remained as much in love as ever.*

*In an instant, they were not old or unfamiliar at all. They were us. I watched Gem and I kissing and holding each other from a distance. No sooner had I wished we were these other versions of ourselves than we became them, already in mid-kiss. It was an immense relief. I pushed myself against her as our mouths grew hungrier, and an intense tingling began between my legs. The more we made out and rubbed against each other, the better I felt.*

I jerked awake.

As usual after a vivid dream, my first thought was, *how much really happened?* and my next was, *none of it, dummy.* It took a few moments longer to believe than usual, maybe because I still had tingles.

"Bad dream?" asked Gem. If I had not been lying down, I would have jumped. There she was, in her signature half-sitting, half-lying position in the armchair, reading as if nothing had happened. Nothing *did* happen, I reminded myself, but I could not shake the feeling something had.

"No. Why?"

"You started moving a little."

"Maybe I'm subconsciously nervous about French." I glanced at the clock and jumped up, though I had over half an hour until my first alarm. "Better get ready."

In the shower, I attempted to calm myself. My heart weighed me down with guilt, like I had been caught masturbating. Actually, I didn't know what that was like, but I thought I might figure it out if I ever had my own room...touching myself, that is, not getting caught. In any case, Gem might feel betrayed if she knew the way I had dreamed about her, but I was not sure if dreams could be wrong. They were mine alone, after all, and I could only control them to a point.

Then again, I had a bigger problem. If I were honest with myself, I had intentionally pushed away thoughts of kissing Gem. They felt taboo. Gem was my best friend, roommate, and confidant all rolled into one, and she had known me since I was little. How could I entertain fantasies about someone like that?

*On the other hand,* I thought as I soaped myself carefully, *how can I not?* She impressed me in every way, and my lack of romantic feelings toward others were at least partially influenced by their comparing unfavorably to her. I didn't just compare their faces or smarts to Gem's, I realized. I compared the way they made me feel, the way she made me smile and my stomach rise in affection, while my peers left me ambivalent. I tried to conjure up an imaginary woman I would rather be with, for a night or for my life, and could not.

There was no use denying it; I had a crush.

I had a crush *on Gem.*

I recalled the concept of Pandora's box from Greek mythology, which I had not studied in over a year. I'd released something inside me, but did it threaten us? I honestly had no idea, but I knew then, if only in the privacy of my own mind, I had turned a corner.

FRENCH PROVED MORE boring than I had anticipated, especially compared to the heady images my hormones had begun to encourage. As both parents had often reminded me, it would look wonderful to get a year ahead on my foreign language requirement this summer, and it would make my schedule less complicated. I had already tested into freshmen-level mathematics and would be walking to the nearby public high school each day; if my French could be raised to that level too, I could stay from lunch until the end of each school day rather than having to hurry back for the last session and still most likely be late.

Convenience aside, a flip through the first few pages of my fresh workbook told me the class would be much harder than the social hour of seventh grade Beginning French. So much for summer relaxation. At least Asha was in the class too; she also hoped to get into high school French, though she hadn't made the cut for math.

For the umpteenth time, the details of my dream marched through my mind with the same determination as its Mardi Gras floats. I would have to learn to make do with compromised concentration, apparently. I shifted in my seat and thanked God, or whomever, I hadn't been born with a penis.

ON THE EVENING of my fourteenth birthday, I waited for a bus to take me to Uptown. I had not had a formal birthday party since my fifth, had developed a queasy stomach at the idea of the stress and expectations. Besides, I knew they were a luxury we could not easily afford, which would put the parents on edge. Though they only talked about money to me on occasion, they fought about it behind their thin bedroom door at least once a month.

Asha had pooh-poohed my party resistance, though, and insisted we at least celebrate over ice cream at McKenzie's Bakery. My stomach rumbled. Perhaps it was not such a bad idea, especially considering I had a feeling she would offer to treat me.

I had only just finished a rare, and rarely matched in awkwardness, turkey dinner with both of my parents. As usual, I had insisted I did not need any presents, which seemed to make them smile upon me approvingly. They always did, anyway, and brought guilt trips to the table with their perfectly wrapped gifts. I now possessed a gift card from Father, which at least should prove useful, even if it was for a popular department store and not a place with books. With Mother, I was less lucky, unwrapping a set of advanced math-related games on CD-ROM. Apparently, she had not checked this passive-aggressive little nudge with the lord of the computer either, judging from how Father pursed his lips. The most painful, yet in a distant corner of my mind, amusing, detail of all lay in the free, attached bonus CD-ROM: *The Wonders of Geology.*

I gave them both stiff hugs, which I had a feeling none of us wanted but they clearly seemed to expect. I thanked them effusively, saying I was at a loss for words. Too bad I wasn't taking a class in drama. Then again, there truly were *not* words for how little I was interested in rocks.

Obviously, the only person I would have wanted a present from was Gem. It wasn't that I wanted her to spend money on me; I just would have enjoyed a physical reminder of our friendship, whatever else she might or might not feel. These fantasies were at least as far-fetched as the rest of them, since of course she could not leave the house in the first place.

At least, being a Saturday, we had had a little more time to talk than usual. Gem gave me an outlet for my frustration with the parents, particularly on days when they went through the motions of a personal relationship we had never shared. As someone whose parent had been a champion in artifice himself, Gem's understanding made me feel my emotions were legitimate. Jill and Asha, on the other hand, changed the subject when I mentioned not being close to my family. Their West Bank and Uptown home existences appeared idyllic. While I knew, intellectually, a richer family did not equal a happier one, my jealous heart struggled to remember it sometimes.

*Speak of the devil.* I hopped off the bus and trotted my way to the Bakery. At the red and white speckled front table, Asha and Jill waited with festive grins and, yes, wrapped gifts. It surprised me a little, since they did not tend to hang out with each other, but if Asha were going to call another friend of mine over, of course it would be Jill. There weren't many options.

I had opened the presents: a novel called *Life After God* from Asha and, less intriguingly, a glittery eyeshadow kit from Jill. Afterward, the three of us dug into a shared Neapolitan sundae, which, as predicted, I did not have to take out my wallet to get. I marveled in our shared, comfortable silence, until Jill pulled her denim purse into her lap and began to smirk mischievously. "I've got one more surprise," she stage-whispered, and pointed the closed top of the bag across the table toward us. Savoring the drama, Jill pulled the zipper open bit by bit to reveal the shine of a long bottle.

"Jesus!" Asha hissed, shooting glances at the disinterested adults at the tables around us. "Is that what I think it is?"

"Fizzy and sweet, just the way I like it." Jill's eyes glinted. "I thought we might toast to Cassie's graduation from the unlucky thirteen. What do you say?"

What *could* I say? It shocked me. Jill had never mentioned drinking, and while I doubted she was as sophisticated about liquor as she now acted, it troubled me that I couldn't take a lack of experience for granted anymore. The idea of partaking with her struck me as wrong, but maybe that was just because the person in my life who drank the most was my father. Asha's eyes went wide, but she didn't tell Jill to stop. Logic stepped in, and finally I asked, "Where would we do it?"

"My place is fine," Asha piped up. "My parents will probably be out all night." The three of us exchanged glances, which I would later come to know as the excitement of children who fancy themselves pushers of boundaries. I suspect we each admired our own daring, on the walk to Asha's, at embarking on a small, forbidden adventure.

"I'VE ONLY KISSED one boy," Jill giggled an hour later. "We played Truth or Dare at camp. He wasn't cute, and it didn't really feel like anything."

"Still one up on me," Asha sighed, eyeing the remnants of the wine bottle. We had each only poured one glass, but the strawberry elixir was already low in the bottle. True, our glasses probably held a little more than an actual wineglass, but I had the feeling both Asha and Jill were acting more inebriated than they were.

"You're kidding!" Jill practically shouted. "I mean, you're so pretty." I jerked my head up, surprised. Could straight girls just say those things without feeling embarrassed or like they were confessing something?

"Tell that to the Beatles. I mean..." Asha broke up laughing. "If they'd never gotten old."

"Or dead!"

"Or dead," she agreed, lifting her empty glass for Jill to clink. I knew I should be pleased they were getting along, but I found myself jealous of their burgeoning connection. Was I that petty? *Maybe,* I thought, *I'm just nervous because I've seen all sorts of trouble happen in trios of friends.* Maybe a part of me wondered if their new camaraderie would lead to secrets and gang-ups.

I realized both of my friends were turned toward me expectantly. "What?"

"What about the birthday girl?" Jill prompted.

"Kissing, you mean? No. Boy count is at zero." Their eyes met and they remained quiet, apparently having already developed telepathy with each other. "What?"

"What about girls?" Asha said softly, studying my face.

"Oh." The familiar flush began creeping up my neck. "No. I've never kissed a girl either."

"But...?" Jill prompted

I rolled my eyes at her. "Are you asking if I'm gay, if the rumors are true? Because it's not like you to be this diplomatic."

She waved her hands. "I'm too drunk for big words!"

I grabbed the bottle and drained the dregs of the sticky-sweet wine, not bothering with a glass. It took longer than I had thought it would. Replacing it with a final clank, I announced, "I do, in fact, like girls."

"Good for you," Asha replied while Jill clapped exaggeratedly.

"But are you bi?"

"Aw, Jill! Leave the girl alone."

"I don't think so." I shrugged. "Boys don't interest me."

"You're lucky. They suck!" And just like that, the conversation moved on, with my dizzy mind dwelling several paces behind it.

I CREPT INTO my dark house, heart jumping at every creak but a happiness hovering inside me. Suddenly, anything felt possible. My footsteps were erratic, and I had to hold the banister to feel sure of my balance. Still, I remembered to skip the noisy final stair, which seemed wonderfully significant, though I did not know of what.

Gem was midway between her chair and the bookcase, finished novel in hand, when I came in. "Have a good time?"

"Actually, I did." This was not something I could say for many social occasions.

"Good—" Gem started, but instinctively, my feet carried me toward her. I studied her adorable face from up close, one piece at a time.

"We're almost the same age now," I murmured.

"S-sort of," she stammered. My feeling swelled within me and I leaned forward, my lips close to hers. Her eyes fluttered shut, I felt her breath on my mouth, and I had never experienced so much excitement at once. But then, her eyes flew back open and she darted away.

"What are you doing?" She spoke quietly but did not seem angry as far as I could tell.

Tears came to my eyes. "I..." I had no idea how to explain myself.

"Cassie?" Gem whispered, her forehead buckling into a frown. "Have you been drinking?"

"A little." I returned her gaze, feeling wild with regret. "I've...never kissed anyone."

"So you want to get it over with," Gem said flatly, backing farther away.

"No! Not at all." The words did not require a decision. I felt them coming, unstoppable. "I love you."

She fixed her gaze on the wall and shook her head, once, twice, four times. "You're drunk."

"I'm not!" I lowered my voice, remembering my parents. "I only had one glass. Well, one and, um, an eighth, maybe? A third? Doesn't matter. I mean what I'm saying, Gem. I've meant it for a long time."

"In a way, maybe. We're like family."

My heart fell. "That's not it!" I snapped in a vicious whisper. "I don't love you like I love my family. I mean, I don't love them, but if I did..." I took a deep breath. "I'm *in* love with you, Gem."

"This isn't right," Gem whispered, as if to herself. Her eyes went everywhere but at me. "Look, you need to go to bed. Drink a few cups of water first. We'll talk tomorrow."

"Gem!" I protested, but she hustled out. I fell onto the bed and released my tears. After several minutes, I switched the lamp off and kicked my way under the covers. *I can't be expected to sleep tonight,* I thought wildly; *I have a broken heart!* But I drifted off in seconds.


MY THIRST HIT me before I opened my eyes, followed in quick succession by my shame. I stumbled to the bathroom, a taste of last night's dizziness hovering on the edges of my vision, and put my mouth under the faucet. The water splashing over my face helped too.

God, was I stupid. I would have given anything to wipe the night clean of my scene with Gem. There was a certain relief in the knowledge she knew of my feelings at last, but I had told her in the sloppiest, most immature way possible. *She'll probably live in the study now,* I figured, *or maybe even in Mother and Father's room! Anything to be away from me.*

I reentered my bedroom to find Gem sitting on my quilt, resolute. My lack of faith in her seemed to have conjured her presence. I shut the door automatically, then realized this might seem presumptuous. I had ruined the ease between us.

"First of all," she began, "what did you and Asha do last night?"

For a strange second, I thought she was asking if we had done anything sexual, then I remembered the fog still retreating from my head. "We had some wine. Jill brought it, actually; Asha invited her too." Gem tilted her head; she knew I never hung out with both of them at the same time. She seemed on the verge of asking about this development, but we both knew she had bigger fish to fry.

"Who took you home?"

"I took the bus."

Gem sighed and rubbed her temples, like a concerned parent. I began to understand why she had said we were like family. "Please don't do that. If you've been drinking, no matter how much, you need to get someone you trust to go back with you, or just sleep over if it feels safe."

"But then I would've had to call—" I stopped myself and waited for her to go on. It took several agonizing seconds.

Finally, she looked me full in the face and asked, "Do you remember everything that happened last night?" I was a terrible liar, and besides, I'd come this far. I nodded. "I'm sorry," she answered.

I blinked, baffled. "Sorry you don't love me back?"

"No...are you saying—"

"I meant what I said, Gem. I still do."

Gem's face had gone blank and lost. "Listen, Cassie, we've known each other a long time. You're probably the best friend I've ever had, and I've really come to care about you. You've become an attractive young woman, but—" Gem studied her hands, clasped in her lap. "I don't think I'd feel right if I got involved with you. I'd feel like I was taking advantage, or like I was just lonely and missing...contact. You're still really young, and sometimes it's like I raised you."

"Are you attracted to me?" I whispered, and Gem flinched.

"That's not relevant."

"What if we'd grown up together?" I asked, emboldened. "What if we were born around the same time and were lifelong friends? We'd still have had an influence on each other, raised each other in a way, but no one would have a problem with us dating then, would they? Besides the homophobes, I mean," I added hastily.

"But we *didn't*, Cassie. The fact is, I've been on this planet a lot longer than you."

"You're still fifteen. And don't say 'sort of;' you *are*. You haven't been on this planet for so long; you've been in a house, a house where no one could see you and you weren't interacting with the world. You may have had more time to think, but you haven't been living. You haven't grown or had adult experiences. You're fifteen," I finished, my voice getting faster, "and someone's in love with you, and I think you're just scared of being vulnerable again." I turned to leave. Stopping in the doorway, I pivoted and added, "And you know what else? I know you almost kissed me last night."

I left her on the bed, deep in thought.


GEM DID NOT come to the bedroom that night. I forced myself not to go searching for her, though I had to dig my nails into my palms, I wanted to so badly. Everything seemed up in the air. All I knew for sure was I was, in fact, in love, and I had done something about it. I felt powerful, mighty, like I had jumped off a cliff. At the same time, I had become more fragile than I could have imagined.

I forgot to set my alarm, and when Mother opened my door and started yelling, something inside me broke. There was no way I could ace a difficult class that summer. "I'm sick!" I shouted, and my mother stumbled back in surprise. God forbid she hear a raised voice other than her own. Remembering something Jill had once said about her older brother, I added, "I think I have mono."

This was the wrong choice for an imaginary ailment, apparently. Mother's eyes darkened. "Have you been *kissing* people?" she snapped. I sighed and shook my head mutely, thinking, *if only*.

I passed by the study several times, sneaking glances at Gem, who seemed lost inside her head. Our eyes met occasionally, but we never spoke, and she did not try to approach me.

When I continued claiming illness the next day, Mother announced she would skip work to take me to the doctor. I knew exactly how the rest of the day would progress, but I let it play out anyway: the tedious bus-hopping to get to the office, the inability for the doctor or her assistants to find anything remotely wrong, the suspicious griping from Mother on the way home about wasted time and money. Realizing I did not want Gem to hear the conversation I had to begin, I turned to Mother just before we reached Dauphine and announced, "I quit."

"What?" For the second time that week, and more than likely the second time ever, I had shocked her.

"I'm not going to take the French class. I can't. It moves too fast, and it's not engaging enough to keep up. I quit."

A rage flared behind her eyes, but she remained quiet until we reached the house. While opening the front door, she turned to me and spoke in a deadly growl. "I had so many hopes for you. It's a shame if you're not bright after all." Though I needed to enter too, she slammed the door just in front of my face.

GEM FINALLY CAME back to the bedroom in the evening. "I heard what your mom said."

I shrugged, nonchalant as if I hadn't been fighting tears for the past few hours. I knew which phone call she must mean, because I had not left the room since I had returned from the doctor's, let alone talked to Mother. I had begun to brace myself for Father's inevitably horrifying round with me when he got home; when Mother iced me without a screaming, Father's turn evened her out. Having them as parents was like spending my childhood stuck in the middle of a sinister seesaw.

Except...I had Gem.

"You don't have to love me," I whispered. "I just want us to be friends again. I can't stand this, not being close to you." Gem bit her lip with a shy smile, and her lips parted as if she were about to speak, but the front door clanged and we both froze.

Within sixty seconds, he was upon me. Crushed against the bed, he pounded my face into the pillow rhythmically, and I fought to breathe deeply. "What the hell is wrong with you?" he screamed, lifting my head up by the neck only to push it into the wall.

"I—"

"Shut your fucking mouth!" His nails against the side of my face broke the skin one by one as his palm pressed against my cheekbone. He shoved his face directly in front of mine, forcing me to watch it vibrate in fury, contorted and purplish red like a beet. "You good for nothing biiiitch!" he roared, letting out his breath in the word as he speckled my face with hot saliva. "We don't make you work! We probably should, but we wanted you to have opportunities!" He pulled my upper half toward him by the hair. "Is even school too much, you ungrateful brat? Move your fat ass," he sneered, smacking my rear end so hard my nose crunched against the wall. He hopped back to his feet, apparently forgetting he had wanted me to move for some reason, and then he took my hand.

*Huh?* I realized, feeling the smallness and smoothness, it was not his after all. Relief flooded my body. I turned and anchored myself in her dripping brown eyes. She was with me. She was there.

"I do love you," Gem whispered. "I love you so much."

He continued to bellow, occasionally punctuating his prolific disgust with a slap, but it ceased to matter. I realized his actual blows did not hurt the way I had always thought they did; the terror made the incidents so painful. With Gem by my side, holding on to me by the fingers, I could stay calm, waiting for a storm's inevitable end.

And when it ended, she turned and held me without a word. For the first time I could remember, I had not cried in front of him, but Gem was sobbing. We lay together with her arms around me, and I knew if I tried to kiss her again, she would allow it. I would not let our first kiss be mistakable for pity, though. I could wait. My body glowed at her touch, until I finally fell asleep, exhausted with emotion and immensely grateful.

AND WAIT I did. I waited through a summer of being insulted for my first genuinely defiant act. I waited through weeks of my mother pleading with me to tell Father I forgave him for the crescent-shaped scabs around my face, while for the first time, he showed the sudden remorse of a nervous, guilty man whose crime had left an obvious mark. I waited through calls with Asha, as I made inadequate explanations for my withdrawal from French and inability to meet her and Jill for more social occasions before my face healed.

I even waited through the chaos of beginning eighth grade and feeling like an alien trotting to high school math each day. The two other junior high students who had tested in just made it worse, because one of them was Leigh, who still refused to acknowledge our history. The class seemed all the more intense since the teacher, Ms. Tucker, was also the high school principal, but even that could not keep my mind off Gem for long.

Waiting, I realize now, was what I needed to do, to make the ocean of my anger subside enough to be in a proper mental state. I did not feel tortured, either, since more than anything physical, I wanted Gem's company, and I had it.

However temporarily, I was in a happy state of mind for Halloween. I returned to an empty home laughing that night. Jill, Asha, and I had found three pairs of plastic caps with Mickey Mouse ears, each bought a set of cheap sunglasses from the gas station, and gone trick or treating as the three blind mice. Half-assed though our costumes were, no one refused us candy, and we had returned to Asha's for newly acquired sugar and Asha's parents' sneakily hidden alcohol.

Actually, I had not partaken of the latter, remembering what Gem had advised. Besides, I had a feeling this would be a good night to have my wits about me. I guess I can call it a hunch.

I entered my bedroom. Gem lay sprawled in waiting across my bed, without a book, just gazing at the ceiling. Our eyes met, she got up to meet me, and without a word, our lips came together. Explosions happened in my head during our long, gentle kiss, after which we wrapped our arms around each other and held each other for a long time.

I was so happy I could have cried.

# Chapter Eight

THE SECOND HALF of junior high turned out not to be miserable after all, largely because I spent it exploring the various pleasures of making out.

I would lick between her lips, eager to taste her tongue and get a feel for the scents inside her mouth each day. She would hesitate just a second, waiting for me to be sure we weren't moving too fast, and I would push her onto the bed and let our lips grow fierce.

In the middle of the night, I would feel her lick my ear and shiver, locking my mouth on hers before I had fully exited my dreams.

"Does this feel wrong to you?" I would whisper, stroking her neck as I lay on top of her across the armchair, one of my thighs between both of hers.

"N-no," she would whisper breathily, and I would grow even more excited at the sound of her voice drugged with desire.

Sometimes I would think of her with Daze, in boarding school rooms I would never see, on a blanket over dirt in total darkness, and be wracked by a hot jealousy. If only I could be her "first" with everything, the way she was for me. While we were together, though, my qualms melted away, because without prior knowledge of her history, I never could have guessed Gem had done all this before. Both of us having denied our feelings for quite a while, Gem, who'd had no romance in decades, was as hungry as I in my first flush of lust. We still had illuminating talks, but inevitably our words would turn into caresses and still more kisses, and by the time they began my palms would have been sweating with want for five minutes or more already.

For the first time, I habitually woke before Gem and would lie stock-still for hours, gazing at her as she slept. Though my sleeping hours had been more satisfying than ever since the beginning of our relationship, or maybe *because* they had, my amazement at having her beside me tended to wake me. The sight of her at peace amazed me since I could not imagine why she needed to sleep in the first place. That detail grew in my mind until one night, I kissed her awake—she liked that—for a gentle question. Understandably, Gem didn't enjoy combating questions about ghostery like an interactive science exhibit, but it had been ages since the last time.

"Why *do* you sleep, anyway?" I asked when we broke from kissing, some time later. "I'd think you might not need to." I was careful to avoid making statements involving the term "human," because, beating heart or no, Gem remained one of those as far as I was concerned.

Gem raised her hands, which fell along either side of me, in a gesture of cluelessness. "I think it's a mind thing. A thinking brain...or, uh, spirit of a brain just can't survive without a break." She leaned against one elbow, her soft hair falling into my face. "I don't really 'get sleepy' the way I used to, though. My first few days after death, I didn't sleep at all, but I realized I missed it, maybe even needed it. I've learned to just relax until the conscious part of me shuts off."

I considered this. "So, basically...you hypnotize yourself."

"I guess."

"Wow." I rolled her below me, savoring the way my weight fell on top of her. On top of her clothes, but still. "So, not only is my girlfriend gorgeous and brilliant; she's a magician."

"Have I worked my magic on *you*?" Gem clapped a hand to her forehead. "Oh, God, I can't believe I said that! Corny! Your girlfriend is *corny* too!"

I tickled her stomach. "Come here, corny lady."

MY GRADES FELL that semester, but I did not care as much as I would have a year before. I still pulled at least a "B" in every subject, and I had already begun a long path of disillusionment with the educational process in general. I did not doubt I would someday go to college, but working through half the night and pinching myself awake in class began to seem, well, not worth it.

I began to see all my parents' pressure on me had a seed in their intense wish to brag. If I chose a university I liked, without a name that could act as a boast in of itself, the only one to lose would be them. Thinking of college at all, in fact, became trying, as I would have to decide whether to leave Gem. Instead, I pushed worries of over four years in the future aside...and focused on Gem and I pushing each other against every wall in the house. I had the love bug, the same one familiar to folks the world over, but unlike my peers, I had the distinct advantage of sharing a home with the object of my affections.

Of course, we were also living with my parents. We rarely left my room unless they were out, and even when they walked past my shut door, we froze and I held my breath. Maybe they would just assume I was dancing if they heard movement; I knew when they heard my voice, they took me to be talking on the cordless phone. Even knowing my parents witnessed evidence of my existence embarrassed me somehow; I spent my meager allowance on snacks because I felt squeamish about eating theirs. At worst, I knew, they would think I was masturbating during my make out sessions with Gem...but even that would be humiliating.

As for my sexuality, Gem and I had technically not done anything my classmates would qualify as beyond *first base* by Christmas break. Sometimes, even I struggled to believe it. Passionately kissing Gem seemed like a more intense sexual experience than anything I had read or seen in the movies, which is not to say I didn't want to do anything else. I knew my first properly sexual experience would be a marker in my life with her, as well as some sort of irrevocable break with my upbringing.

When my hands traveled too much, though, Gem pushed me away. "You're young," she scolded once in November, though her reluctance to stop was clear.

"*You* were fourteen."

"Well, yeah, but...let's just take it slow, okay? We've only been together a month, and we've got plenty of time."

At first, I worried her reluctance stemmed from technical concerns. What were the limitations of a ghost's body? Asking seemed rude at best, so I tried to broach the topic as casually as possible.

"Are you sure it'll be, you know, the same for you?" I tried to ask as if I had only scientific curiosity. "I mean, you can't go to the bathroom—"

"I can," she corrected. "If I think about it, I still can. I just don't want to. Same with throwing up. I think it has to do with, uh—" She turned her head away. "Body memories." My cheeks heated up when I realized what she meant. Did that mean I should be thankful to Daze, even as I resented her? "And it won't be *the same*," she hastened to add, "because it'll be with you."

It seemed unfair. I had never seen Gem in a state of even partial undress when she had seen me in my underwear countless time. These days, of course, I forwent stepping into the bathroom to change, which sometimes provoked renewed kissing with only several scraps of clothing over my body. Her arm trailing over my bare stomach was so agonizing, it surprised me I never had a bruise.

I wanted nothing more in the world than to unbutton her Boy Scout shirt. When I asked outright, while we had been hot and heavy for more than an hour, she refused. "We're not there yet."

"I'm not asking to go, you know, *all the way*."

"And what does that mean, anyway?" I realized I didn't know, considering we were both girls. "That's what I thought," Gem proclaimed, though I had not spoken aloud. "Personally, I don't think there's such a thing as 'all the way,' or maybe it's different for everyone. People like different things, and if you're doing something sexual, why rank what it is? This applies to hetero couples too, by the way. People pretend sex is more cut-and-dry than it is. Like most things." Gem may have been my first romantic partner, but no one else could have expanded my mind at a moment like that.

CHRISTMAS ARRIVED, PROVIDING me with a heaping dose of my special festive ambivalence. String lights, decked-out trees, and holiday music made my heart rise, but the actual holiday tended to be less pleasant, with its emphasis on family and a religious background less subtle than a lot of people seemed to have convinced themselves.

My mother tended to overspend on gifts Father and I did not want, which led to weeks of screaming arguments between them about money. While it was a relief to hear them yelling at each other rather than at me, those options were becoming the only two activities my parents seemed to consider each day, and this depressed me. It all seemed so tedious. If they didn't have enough work to occupy themselves, couldn't they make some friends or pick up a hobby?

Christmas Eve had the worst of it, as usual. I maneuvered myself into a shiny red dress Jill had bought for me. Though I rarely dressed up, I had to admit it was beautiful and made me feel attractive too. Gem rarely commented on my clothes, but she said this had nothing to do with whether she liked them. On occasion, Gem assured me she did, in fact, find me lovely, but overemphasizing the fact demeaned my other great qualities. This was a trap, Gem claimed, into which many couples fell. I could see her point, but I also could not deny my pleasure when I turned to her, slinky in red, and her mouth fell open.

Minutes later, Mother opened the door, gave me a once-over, and made an exclamation of disgust. She hurried to my closet to rifle through it without my permission, and shoved a jacket at me, asking, with a glare, if I wanted everyone to think she had raised a "tart." Maybe no scene could be perfect...though the word "tart" made me think of pricey local pastry shops more than anything. I retaliated by fantasizing on the bus ride to the church: Gem admiring me in a display window, slapping down a few dollars, and carrying me away to devour me. I shivered once, and Mother broke my daydream to congratulate herself out loud on her jacket recommendation.

I couldn't focus on any of the service's negligible variations for the year. It was like watching a strange ritual from a distance. They introduced a new leader for the children's choir, and I found I had already forgotten the previous one. I couldn't help but judge myself a failure for not buying into the magic of Jesus. I stayed awake by fingering the contents of my purse. If I wanted to worry, I had more immediate matters for which to do so.

"SO, HOW WAS church?"

"How do you think?" I chuckled nervously, and, without further ado, I pulled the gift, in crumpled wrapping, out of my bag. "I say we have a merry Christmas anyway, Gem."

"What's this?" She bounced off the bed and pulled the small item from my hand.

I took a deep breath and spoke through the knot in my throat. "I tried to find something worthy of you." Gem was beginning to look misty-eyed, herself. "I found nothing, and all the ideas I had relating to your past were sad, of course. I knew you wouldn't care about the money, anyway. You would want something personal."

I nodded at her to go ahead and open it. Gem pulled out the bracelet I had woven, with hearts in every color of the rainbow and both of our names in red. "I know it's kind of childish, but I wanted something you could always keep with you, and that didn't have to show...because if it did, my parents could see it floating, right?"

"I'm not sure." She smiled, twirling it around in her hand. "But it's adorable."

"Have a seat." Gem situated herself on the bed and I tied the gift around her ankle, letting it fall beneath her boot before I met her eyes again. "Merry Christmas, love."

Gem kissed me hard, one hand weaving through my hair, pulling lightly, the other around my waist. I could not remember, even the next morning, which of us had pushed or pulled the other onto the bed first, but by the time we fell onto my comforter together, I knew that night, that chilly, Christmas night, would be different from our nights of cuddling. I knew we were both ready to move forward and our love for each other would move us there organically.

Afterward, as I lay in her arms thinking of all we had to look forward to, she murmured, "This is the first time I've been naked in decades. I think I've been hiding from my human body." Though unsure of what she meant, I wept at her bittersweet words, and we fell asleep in a heady cloud of emotions, holding each other tight.

IN THE FOLLOWING months we spent much time in each other's arms, or making love, or both. Every day brought thrilling new romantic moments, even when they were only words. We fit so much into the short, hard-won tenure I wondered later if some reptilian part of my brain had known we would be separated.

Still, in the worst moments of the time that came next, it was most often Christmas Eve I remembered.

# PART TWO

# Chapter Nine

THE INCIDENT BEGAN with the type of petty school drama I had always avoided.

I trekked to the high school for Trigonometry with an extra dose of butterflies in my stomach. The rest of my finals had provided no trouble, but if I did not do well today, I knew I might not pass the class. While I would still be ahead of most ninth graders if I repeated the course the following year, I wasn't sure prestigious colleges would overlook a "D" on a middle school transcript.

In any case, I could not have studied any harder. I had even, with great reluctance, told Gem I needed the bed to myself, to rule out distractions from a good night's worth of sleep. After that day, I planned to make it up to her.

In the past few months, we had never gone for more than a few days between sexual sessions, save once. The unfortunate break had occurred after Mother had opened the door on us, and I had wondered if what I felt was similar to the first phases of a heart attack. So far as I knew, she had neither seen nor suspected anything; Gem had been below me, face between my legs under the covers, and it must have seemed as if I were simply on my back in bed, preparing for a nap.

Still, it had shocked the hell out of me, and naturally, the mood had gone. For two weeks after, while I could not resist a good amount of kissing with Gem, I had been petrified to go any further lest Mother's obnoxious, clueless face intrude on our room again. Eventually, of course, the terror had worn off as the temptation of our love flared up.

*No more thinking about Gem right now,* I chided myself, as I grew situated at the desk and held my pencil at the ready.

During the exam, I became so focused it took me a while to even hear Grace's furtive whispers.

"Hey!" When I registered the disturbance, my eyes went from hers to the folded paper in her hand, then to my left at Leigh, and my heart fell. Grace glanced at Ms. Tucker, who still appeared riveted in her grading, and extended the arm with the paper.

I shook my head before I realized I had moved at all. "It's for Leigh," she breathed, as if that would hold any sway. When I shook my head again, Grace cut her eyes at me and threw it, like a paper airplane, directly at me. Startled, I put up my hands and deflected the note, which angled several rows forward. All around the room, heads snapped up, including Ms. Tucker's.

AFTER SPEAKING TO each individually, Ms. Tucker addressed the three of us from behind a giant desk, sitting uncomfortably close in her tiny office. Again, I had been seated between Leigh and Grace, and I could feel the fury radiating from each side.

"Your stories all contradict each other, which is typical in these matters," she began, "but based on what I saw and the article itself, I have a pretty good idea of what happened." The "article" concerned sat, unfolded, on the desk between us. It began with a fancily written "Leigh" and a colon. I bit back a smile.

"Cassandra, policy mandates I inform your parents of the incident today. I will let them know you're not in trouble yourself. As for the two of you," she finished, head shaking back and forth from my left to my right, "I'm afraid I'll be seeing you next year."

Relief and fear coursed through me in a confused concoction, and my body, late to the game, began to shake. It seemed like an eternity until Ms. Tucker cleared her throat and added, "You may go, Cassandra." When I reached the doorway, I made the mistake of turning back. Leigh's head rested in her hands, but Grace's eyes locked onto me, glaring. She glanced back at Ms. Tucker, who was indeed scrutinizing her. Apparently deciding she did not care, Grace drew a finger across her throat.

WHEN THE FINAL bell rang, I fought the urge to sprint back to the bus stop. Anyone who had ever cared to notice would know I usually walked through the front of the campus, so instead I opted for an exit via the back field. The humidity pressing in from all sides made me dizzy, but I would push on. I had still not decided on an evasive route home when I heard her voice.

"Hey, if it isn't the dyke lady." My stomach fell. I spun around to see Grace gliding toward me, and by her side, Leigh. Like on the first day of seventh grade, our eyes met briefly, and I could have sworn I saw something vulnerable. An instant later, she had set her jaw. "Beat up any make out partners lately? Or are you too busy ratting out your peers?"

"I—"

"Make out partners? No one would kiss her," Leigh chimed in. Too late, I realized Grace had situated herself on the opposite side of me in case I tried to run.

"I didn't mean anything; I swear! I didn't know—"

"Takes a true narc," Grace continued, ignoring me, "to turn on your own sleepover bud." She spoke with such derision, both Leigh and I stumbled back a step. *So, Leigh remembers me,* I realized, *and she doesn't say hello...but does talk to someone else about our old friendship?*

"Not sleepovers! Jesus!" Leigh sputtered. "We just played! I mean, yeah, she wanted to have sleepovers, but I told my mom she creeped me out. I knew what she wanted."

"Oh, for God's sake, Leigh!" I erupted. "We were only, like, six! We never even talked about sleepovers."

"So, are you denying you're a dyke, as well as a narc?" Grace stepped closer. Her hand slipped out of her blazer pocket cupped around a red plastic lighter. For the first time, I realized how secluded we were, how few rules governed the shrinking space between us.

*All I have to do is get away from them,* I thought. My heart hammered, but my brain remained very still. *All I have to do is make them leave, and then I can start my summer and be with Gem and never talk to these awful girls again.* I stared Grace in the face and replied, "I'm 'also denying' who I am is any of your business."

"Sassy!" Grace spat. "You'll never snag a girl with that attitude."

"Good! I have someone, anyway."

"Leigh, am I hearing this? Could it be? Queers in love?" Grace did a grotesque imitation of a swoon. Leigh straightened up, emboldened at the sound of her name. "Who's the lucky bitch? Is she pretty? And, ugh, I'm not sure I want to know, but...does she put out?"

"Shut the hell up."

"I'm sure she's ugly." Leigh rolled her eyes. "And probably dumb as shit. She'd be pretty jealous to know you were with us, huh?"

"No!"

"Well, let's give her something to be jealous about," Leigh taunted, grabbing the collar of my blouse and yanking me close to her. "Give us a kiss, dyke!"

Adrenaline flooded through my body. My hands were a blur.

When Leigh wailed like a banshee, clutching her arm, her noises tearing through our crafted society like paper, my body went rigid, but my mind seemed to float away. I hovered just above the gruesome scene, outside my flesh but eerily calm. She had insulted my love, my identity, and I had retaliated in the only way I could have. I doubted any man could have hurt me like she had.

But when the sisters, and later, the headmaster, rushed out, they didn't see Leigh's attacks on Gem. They didn't see Grace's escalating threats or the neat line of inevitability. They saw nothing but me, turned toward them in the middle of the field, frozen and slack-jawed, with a fist still clenched around a switchblade dripping with guilt.

# Chapter Ten

I WADED THROUGH the next few days in shock. Maybe it's more accurate to say I was dragged. I was only intermittently present in scenes of the aftermath. Everything appeared through a warped wall of glass, and words sounded underwater.

The places through which adults dragged me included inside a police station, numerous car interiors, and the headmaster's office several times, surrounded by dark, locked school buildings. They took me to my house, which I could barely recognize. I heard myself speak a few times, but my consciousness seemed far away. Five repeated words, like a mantra: "I had to do it." Several times, my voice said something that sounded like "Gem." *No*, I thought. *No, no, no,* but the command floated away in a bubble that dispersed before reaching my vacant body.

I did not try to process my parents' screams into words. I'm still unsure of what they said. I am sure it would have made no difference.

Gem finally broke through by shouting in a way that would have enraged my mother had she been able to hear her. "Can't you just tell me what happened? Talk to me, please! For fuck's sake, I love you! I'm scared!"

For the first time in two days, I met someone's eyes. "I stabbed her," I whispered. "I stabbed a girl. Leigh."

Gem clapped a hand over her mouth and eased herself onto the bed. "Oh, God," she whispered, and the first wave of shame and regret washed over me. The incident had been so brief; I could hardly believe it had changed the course of my life. Leigh and Grace were nothing but two insecure kids who should have held no sway on my future. "Is she dead?" I strained to think over everything, trying to make sense of the shapes and hollers that had surrounded my unresponsive senses.

"No. Her arm. It was just her arm." Mother, I realized, had offered to pay for Leigh's stitches when her irate parents approached, and I could not remember any further discussion about her condition. Most of the talk so far, I realized, be it involving parents, school officials, or police, had focused on me.

"Are you going to juvie?" Gem's hands trembled, and that scared me more than anything.

"I don't know..." I began, but I stopped when she buried her head in the blanket, shaking it back and forth fiercely. She reminded me of a movie I had secretly watched at Jill's about possession, with a convulsing child who had been wracked with a demon.

"They can't!" she wailed. "They can't take you. I won't let them. Oh, God, not you..." The door opened inward from behind me, throwing me to the ground and startling us both.

"Get in the car," Father muttered woodenly. When I hesitated, he dragged me by the collar, like Leigh had. We moved away from Gem's horrified face.

"AS I MENTIONED before, the punishment for violent incidents is usually expulsion," the headmaster began, his round, childish face in a rare grave expression. "However, your daughter has already finished her finals. She has no coursework left to do, so while we could withhold the diploma, Cassandra would still have legally finished junior high. Honestly, bringing a weapon to school is grounds enough for expulsion; it is completely not allowed."

I waited for my father to clarify: he had told me to always carry the blade. Father did not speak. "The police will likely sentence her to a reform facility for some time, considering the violent nature of her crime."

That was it, then: I *would* go to juvenile hall. I could not imagine surviving months without Gem, and I knew my being sent away would bring up painful memories for her too.

But then, the smug man went on.

"Frankly, what concerns me the most is not even the violence. It's her delusions, and, uh...what they may imply about her real life." When he narrowed his eyes in my direction, it was the first time he had acknowledged my physical presence at all. "Tell us, Cassandra," he said in a sing-song mock, "do you have anything more to sat about Gem?"

Time seemed to stand still. I feared I'd sink through the chair. *I talked about Gem? Oh, lord...did I mention we have sex?*

Again addressing my parents, he said, "Now, I didn't want to get into this before, because I wanted to make sure I was remembering the right girl. I've confirmed I was, and I'm sorry to have to share this."

Standing, he approached a gargantuan filing cabinet against the right wall. A drawer clanged open, and the headmaster reached into its jammed-full contents and removed a plastic envelope with paper inside, so adeptly I knew he had practiced the gesture. He removed two papers from the plastic and handed them to my parents, who stood like executioners behind me, avoiding my eyes. One lined paper held a teacher's blue scrawl in a paragraph visible from the back side, and the other was half-lined and half-white, with no ink bleeding through. "You see," the headmaster whispered with a hint of triumph, "her delusions started early."

Surprising everyone, I sprung out of my chair and grabbed both papers.

The half-lined one was familiar. The composition sheet's upper half depicted a crayon drawing of a girl with brown hair and a diamond pattern across her legs. The other contained heated, accusatory notes from my second-grade teacher.

I continued to stare as the man spoke. "Don't cry, dear lady," he cooed to my mother. "We know people who can help your child." I thought I might fade into the murk of the last few days again, but the headmaster's next words were loud and clear: "We've dealt with situations like this before."

THEY HAD ME wait in a tiny room attached to the kindergarten classrooms; I could only assume it existed for time-outs. This was apropos, I suppose, since I had violated the rules of life by which the headmaster and my parents lived. Then again, I had really been doing so for a long time.

It alarmed me that the anger over my stabbing Leigh, a genuine crime, seemed to have subsided. I was ready to atone for what I had done with the knife, even if Grace and

Leigh never paid at all. Then again, this made a perverse kind of sense. Violence was par for the course in their world. Lesbianism and ghosts were not.

Remembering Leigh's horrified shrieks, my regret nearly knocked me over. She had behaved appallingly, but most of my peers would have done the same. Under enough pressure, even Jill might use homophobic language. Leigh was selfish, but her selfishness was a type I could understand. Had I had a few moments to think about the situation, I would have known she would not actually force a kiss onto me; that'd be damning to her. She probably wouldn't have hit me either, letting Grace take care of it, in which case the switchblade would have stayed safely in my pocket. Grace did not trigger the same emotions Leigh did, and I had acted out of pure instinct. I would have to ask my parents, or any of the adults pulling the strings in this scenario, about her state, to be sure she was okay.

The door flew open with a wooden pop, presenting a large woman with burgundy hair and completely black attire. "I'm Roxanne," she said, with a smile and an extended hand. "You must be Cassandra. I've been hearing about you from a lot of people, but I've been hoping to hear how you would describe yourself."

This seemed an auspicious start. "Well, I'm fourteen, fifteen soon. I like to read a lot, and I do pretty well in school." I fidgeted, unused to being in the spotlight. "I don't know what else to say."

"You have a girlfriend, from what I understand."

My heart beat faster. "Um, yes. I mean...I don't remember what I said after—after what happened with Leigh. I think I might have been in shock. I'm gathering I upset some people."

"Leigh is the student with whom you had a fight?"

"Yes." I began to relax a little. It did not sound so bad when she put it like that. "Earlier, she and her friend got caught cheating on a test, and they thought it was my fault. They started threatening me, Leigh grabbed me, and I took out the switchblade...which Father has me carry," I couldn't resist adding.

"I see." Roxanne flipped through a folder on her lap. "Well, fights like this have been known to happen amongst kids your age, especially in New Orleans. The carrying of weapons is more common than most of us would admit, and I understand your schoolmate's wound is minor." That answered one nagging question, thankfully. "Unfortunately, without a witness, we cannot confirm she physically accosted you first."

"I understand. But...did you talk to Grace?"

"I did not, personally, but I see the police did. In fact, it says you were in the room..." She glanced up at me, eyebrows knit together. "You don't remember?" I shook my head. "According to the report, Grace stated you had attacked Leigh unprovoked, to which you said she was lying and had, and I quote, 'talked shit about my girlfriend.'"

I winced. I had picked a great time to unleash my secret potty mouth. "I don't remember saying that, but yes, it's true. First, they were angry about the test, but then they started calling me a dyke, saying my girlfriend must be stupid, things like that."

"She's not, I'd assume." It took me a moment to figure out about whom she was speaking. "From what I hear, you're a bright girl, and I wouldn't expect you to be dating a so-called stupid person."

I began to thaw, my shoulders relaxing. This Roxanne really seemed to like me. "She's not." I smiled. "She's very smart."

"Why don't you tell me about her?" I stiffened up visibly. "Cassandra, I'm here to help. What you tell me stays within these walls, and I promise you, I've heard it all by now. Nothing will seem weird to me, or even impossible."

I felt the weight of my situation, of my own despair, and I told her.

I told her everything.


TWENTY MINUTES LATER, Roxanne called in both of my parents and the headmaster. The smile dropped from her face as if she had been wearing a mask. "I'm afraid it's very serious," she announced. "Not only is Cassandra suffering from homosexuality; as you suspected, sir, she persistently sees a ghost. The girl even believes she has a relationship with one."

My mouth went dry as the expressions of horror traveled through their little semicircle. Mother dissolved into choking wails, as if she had been told she was dying. "All I ever wanted was for you to be normal, Cassandra!"

I snapped out of my stupor. "Really, *Mom*?" We were both aware of the absurdity in my calling her that, and it seemed to sting. "Didn't you want me to beat out everyone academically, and never get in trouble, and make you look like a perfect parent?" I whirled around, seething. "And *you*!" I pointed at Roxanne, if that was indeed her name. "You said what I told you was confidential! I thought you were some sort of counselor!"

"I am, dear," she replied, and now her soft tone seemed sinister and condescending. "I said your secrets would stay within these walls, which they have." Obscenely, she dared to chuckle. I could hardly believe she had played a wording game on me; was she six? "Besides," she added, her eyes darkening, "I'm not legally obligated to keep the confidence of criminals."

My mouth went dry. "Roxanne—"

"You may address me simply as 'Ma'am.' And now, I'm afraid you'll have to come with me. We have no time to waste in your case."

EVEN IF MA'AM had managed to coax information out of me, she would not talk me into her van. She had to call out two guards, both men, from the backseat to maneuver me inside, while my parents and the headmaster stood idly by. "There's nothing wrong with me!" I shouted as the sliding door closed. "Help!" Mother and Father stood side by side, not touching and certainly not helping, locked in their own private, mental hells as their daughter was taken away. They did not even give me a chance to go home for clothes or other personal items, let alone to give Gem a proper, though indubitably temporary, goodbye.

We did pass through Dauphine Street, though, directly past the house. This may have been a deliberate tactic orchestrated by Ma'am to shatter my heart and leave me as vulnerable as possible. I strained the muscles in my forearms yanking at the door handle, though of course they had master-locked it. Finally, I pressed my face to the closed window shouting, "Gem! *Gem!*"

In retrospect, I hope she did not see me. After all, I was headed into a twisted torture similar to some of the hardships of her own short life. The pain over seeing my desperate, soaked face is more than I ever would want her to bear.

"YOU'RE GOING TO need to look at me eventually," Ma'am snapped. The room only allowed about five feet between our chairs, but I twisted my head as far away as I could. Her tone softened, and for a second she returned to the charismatic persona from the time-out room. "We want to help you, Cassandra, but we're going to need a little cooperation on your part."

"Still?" I hissed. Maybe it was wishful thinking, but I could have sworn she flinched.

"I understand if you feel betrayed."

"How very perceptive you are." I had never been much for sarcasm, but I could think of no more appropriate occasion to use it.

She sighed. "I have pathos for your situation, Cassandra; you can hardly imagine. When I was about your age, I was dating a ghost too."

I started and turned back to her, despite myself. Perhaps I had again misjudged this situation.

"Yes, it's true," she continued. "After I turned sixteen, not much older than you, I saw an eighteen-year-old boy approach me at my aunt's house. She walked directly through him. With a little research, I discovered he was the same boy who had been in a fatal car accident the previous week. He told me he had the ability to enter several of the surrounding houses, but as we came to talk more, he took to spending all of his time at my aunt's. I, in turn, spent most of my time there with him."

I studied her face as she went on; my intuition told me this story was not a spontaneous invention. Then again, look where my intuition had landed me so far. "Soon, we agreed we were dating. He had been quiet and bookish in his life but opened up to me. He proved a great listener, and we had a lot in common, having attended the same high school. He created art for me out of my aunt's recycled magazines. Within a year, I had invented an excuse to spend some of my nights there, and we began, so to speak, to make love."

The thought of Ma'am lost in love, waking up with her arms around someone, warmed me all over in spite of myself. "He sounds wonderful. Why did you let him go?"

"He didn't exist."

My heart fell. A rude awakening. "What do you mean?"

"Just what I said: he didn't—doesn't—exist. There are no ghosts. We create them out of our own loneliness and our mental illnesses, and someday, no one will have to remind you of this anymore." Loss bloomed behind her eyes, but her expression had tightened into steel. "Believing in your companion is an abomination to God, the Bible, and the very concept of heaven."

I shook my head in disgust. The pattern in this conversation had become clearer. "So, what? You think you just imagined him?"

"I don't 'think' anything, Cassandra. I know, without a doubt, that my dissatisfaction with my godless life fabricated a charlatan savior in my mind. My ghostly boyfriend was an invention of mine, and I wanted to believe in him so much I subconsciously erased my memories of reading about the accident earlier. What I needed, Cassandra—what we all need—is God."

Part of me knew there would be no fruit in arguing with her, but I could not resist.

"So, you were speaking and having sex with...who, then? With the air? Or...with God, maybe?"

"Blasphemous girl!" she snapped and made a visible effort to calm herself. She raised and lowered both her hands, as if conducting a symphony, or the ocean. "I was...consorting with no one. Something happened to damage me, probably early in my life. Perhaps it grew out of dissatisfaction with my father. In any case, I was sick, and so are you; so are all of my patients from around this great country. It is impossible to be happy while behaving sinfully, and that includes having interactions you believe are with a ghost. Such a lifestyle can only lead to unhappiness."

I knew I should keep my mouth shut and not rock the boat, but my years of staying quiet about Gem, and my intense connection with her, had built up inside me into a mountain of pent-up defiance. "I'm going to have to disagree. Gem and I are really, extremely happy."

"You're not happy! You only think you are. Some would call you a lost cause. Fortunately, we here at Chose People Ministries don't believe in such a thing. Your process of conversion therapy will begin tomorrow."

I was too stuck on the name at first to process the important part. "Is this a Jewish group?" Ma'am scowled at me, uncomprehending. "'Chosen People?'" I prompted.

"Chose. The Chose People are us, humankind. We're the only beings God has infused with true, sentient life, and certainly the only beings we should be with in a romantic sense. Simply put: God chose people."

"Oh, God," I whispered, putting my head in my hands. Lightning quick, a sharp pain seared my arm, and

I jerked back up. Ma'am wielded a ruler. Dumbfounded, I stared.

"We do not tolerate such talk. Now," she said, getting up to exit the room, "I'll find guards to escort you to your room. You had best spend today getting your rest," she added darkly. "You'll need it."

STRANGELY—OR PERHAPS not, since all prisons rely on the same basic tactics—the center looked similarly to how I had imagined Gem's boarding school. Pat-downs, they informed me, might happen at any time, "for everyone's protection," without even the relief of staying same-sex. A high fence surrounded the property from all sides. It appeared unclimbable, but to be sure, they had topped it with barbed wire.

On the other hand, I knew Gem's school had been composed of many different buildings between its dorms and classrooms. I was hungry for the wide-open spaces those captured students had had outside.

And, of course, I doubted we would be given enabling drugstore runs.

Chose People Ministries lay entirely in one building, which wound around into a roughly square pattern. Standing on my toes, I peered through the rare window we passed as the guards led me through the labyrinthine connected rooms. There about three windows pointing into the little space in the center of the square to each one window pointing outward, toward nothing but the fence. The middle space was only a grassy area with two meager trees and a bench on either side, like a sad nook for hospital patients who wanted to feel they were part of the outside world.

A guard followed my gaze and announced the Free Area—a name which made me bite my tongue to keep from rolling my eyes—existed only for subjects with advanced progress. I recalled a person could actually die from a lack of exposure to sunlight and wondered if that was their plan.

My room had a window, though, a tiny circle with bars over it, like something out of an old movie. I knew it was a bedroom only because of a mattress with a thin white blanket; it had no other furniture. "You're lucky to get a single room," one hulking man informed me. Behind us, his comrades trudged back out of the door through which we had come in. "That's rare for a newcomer. The issue is, someone with your, uh, perversions can't be left alone with a roommate. Make no mistake, though." He shoved one beefy finger in my face, and I thought of my father. "Your sickness won't get you rewards, queer."

I spun around, wanting to believe I had misheard. I only caught a glimpse of him, face coated in disgust, before the door slammed. I lay down, as exhausted as I could remember being, but most of all wanting unconsciousness to relieve me from this terrible day. I forced my mind to stay as blank as it could, though I could not help but wonder if the process resembled what Gem did each night.

AND THAT IS how I came to be enclosed within alternately padded and metal walls, alone even when others surrounded me. Despite the mockery, the words, the essential torture, I decided I would persevere through the rest of the year. I would not let them break me. I would lie, maybe for the first time in my life, and tell them what they wanted to hear. The folks seemed too worshipping of their own success, regardless of which religion they claimed to follow, to doubt me if I didn't let the armor crack.

Then I would be allowed to go home, which for me meant into Gem's arms.

# Chapter Eleven

A SHREWD, COMPACT bald man in a lab coat appeared by my bed at seven o'clock the following morning. I opened my eyes and recoiled at the sight of him. With his beady eyes, tiny circular glasses, and dewy cheeks, he reminded me of a salamander. As he escorted me through room after interconnected room, I had the feeling of walking through a chain of futuristic boxes; it was like a dream I had had once.

We entered a makeshift kitchen, with a square-shaped metal table, a cluster of folding chairs, and a refrigerator, but nothing to provide heat. In the eerie quiet, I wondered if the other kids were still asleep. The light from the inward window glowed faint and blue, making the fluorescent lights above us seem even brighter.

One guard whom I had not seen before handed me a single string cheese and an apple. "Eat up." I eyed the foods, wondering if the apple had been rinsed off first, then, feeling stupid, contemplating whether they would drug me. In any case, I would have to eat eventually. I bit into the fruit, the red skin thick and rubbery. I might as well appear cooperative right off the bat.

As I soon learned, it was too late for that.

Dr. Salamander, as I began to call him in my mind since the Ministries did not seem to adhere to the quaintness of names, wasted no time. He led me farther down the hall than I had ever been and unlocked a thick door. The guard followed us inside.

This room was just as sparse as the others, but the blue dental chair in its center made it feel more like a doctor's office. Elsewhere, I saw only a clunky projection machine, like the one the Academy had wheeled between classrooms for biology videos. Nodding toward the chair, Dr. Salamander situated himself at the far side of the room and opened his briefcase. I positioned myself in the chair, trying to sit up, stay alert, and fight the urge to recline. *He's not here to fix my teeth*, I reminded myself. But what was this all for?

From the chair, I had a better angle from which to look inside the case. It was not a bag of supplies at all but a portable switchboard of knobs and tiny green screens. Three thick cords in primary colors lay coiled against its machinery.

"You've been labeled particularly resistant," Dr. Salamander announced, eyes still on his tools. "We're here to cure you of your delusions."

"I'm sorry," I lied. "It just surprised me when they brought me in. I don't want to—"

"Quiet." The steel in his single word scared the excuses back down my throat. He moved toward me, unwinding the yellow cord. One end disappeared into the switchboard; the other forked into two thinner wires topped with gauzy pads. His hands landed on either side of my head without him ever meeting my eyes. *He's bored*, I realized as he pulled the papery tape out of his coat pocket and fastened the pads between my eyes and ears. *This is just a job.*

Dr. Salamander nodded at the guard behind me, who had been so still I had forgotten he was there. The guard flicked the projector on. I studied its square, yellowy light against the wall as Dr. Salamander began adjusting his switchboard.

I don't remember what images they chose for the first day. I'm not even sure my eyes were open. The sides of my head were itchy, and then warm, and then numb with pins and needles. Then, everything was electricity, tremors and tingles as my heart jackhammered, blood surging throughout every chamber of my body.

AFTER I HAD been shocked to the point at which I felt dizzy and confused even with the machine off, Dr. Salamander had me repeat cruel words to his satisfaction. "She doesn't exist. My ghost is not real." On that first occasion, I only had to say it three times. I focused on the sounds, the movements of my mouth, and let my mind go totally blank.

Only then did he release me back to my room. I had played my part as I had planned, but honestly, I doubted most patients needed to have gone in with a plot of disguise. I would have said anything to get away from him. My feelings weren't, couldn't be, the point.

On the march back to my room, my feet seemed to wobble on the floor. We passed through the kitchen-box, where four people now sat around the metal table: two girls and a boy around my age and one much younger boy. Apparently, we were interrupting their lunch, but curious as I may have been about the other so-called patients, I was mostly exhausted. I could not have participated in their semblance of a social ritual even if I had been allowed.

As we approached my little room, I remembered a sequence I had read in *The Bell Jar*. The guards halted in surprise when I turned around. "I thought electroconvulsive therapy was only for depressed people."

One grinned. Though the guards were hard to tell apart, with their pale skin, shaved heads, and bodies thick with muscle, his sporadic teeth signaled him as the same man who had called me a queer. "That wasn't ECT, honey," he gloated, "but in case it's news, you *are* depressed. No one can be happy when they've strayed so far from God's plan." He gave me a mocking pat on the head, and I turned away until the door had closed behind them.

# Chapter Twelve

I MET THE other patients the following day. It feels generous to the higher-ups to call them that; *inmates* might be more accurate. Time slowed to such a sickening crawl, it amazed me it managed to pass at all. Without Gem, or at least a book, sleeping was the best activity available to me. It was, then, with some relief that I let myself be led to the table, for my mind as well as my stomach. The guards walked away with the obligatory growled warning to return to my room within an hour.

"Hi, I'm Palace." A tall girl with an accent I couldn't place extended her hand. "You must be Cassandra."

"Cassie, please. Call me Cassie." Perhaps it was foolish considering my recent mishaps, but I liked her immediately. "It's...nice to meet you."

"Likewise." She nodded at the other folks situated around the table in turn, ending with the little boy. "Alvarez, Jenika, and Peter." She leaned back. "Settle a score for us: female or male?"

"Huh?" I glanced at my body and touched my hair self-consciously. While I had sometimes admired the more androgynous folks in New Orleans, I had never considered myself one of them. "I'm a girl."

"I figured. I meant, which gender is your friend?"

"My...oh." I glanced between the four of them dizzily, wondering if I had acquired an understanding I had never before had. "She's a girl too."

"I *knew* it!" Palace pumped her fist into the air in a victory gesture. Her arm was limp, so more an ironic gesture than actually joyful.

"Shh..." Jenika cautioned, eyes darting back and forth. "They'll hear you."

Palace turned her away, essentially shrugging her off, and Jenika returned to the sandwich on her plate. Jenika was plain and had a pale, vacant face, as if something had been defeated at her core. "I thought so," Palace said, and her voice had indeed grown much softer, "because they took you to the torture chamber on your first real day. Those two," she went on, tilting her head at Alvarez and Jenika, "have opposite-sex partners, and their treatments are not as bad. It's not much of a mystery, what *really* concerns them."

"Really?" I whispered, when I really wanted to say, *Can I really trust you?*

"Damn it, Palace," Alvarez hissed, carefully keeping his voice low as well, "it's no picnic for us. We still get the big shocks at least twice a month. Don't play Oppression Olympics just 'cause they think you're gay."

"Did I say it was fun for you?" Palace snapped. "I hate it when you say stuff like that. I'm not after pity, just stating facts."

"Hold on now." I took my chair in front of a peanut butter and jelly sandwich I was no longer sure my stomach could handle. "You're all dating ghosts?" The child, Peter, whose presence I had already forgotten, jumped up, slamming his chair against the table before he hurried away. After a few seconds, I realized my mouth sat ajar.

"Don't worry." Jenika startled me with a hand on my arm. "You didn't do anything wrong. He's just been really traumatized." Her eyes, still distant, were brimming with tears.

Palace went quiet for a minute before saying, "To answer your question, Cassie, no. We're not all dating ghosts. I just have one as a friend, myself, and same with Pete. They don't believe us, though. The Ministry thinks ghosts just use people to defile them for their future hetero spouses."

"But...they don't believe the ghosts are real. Do they?"

"That's the party line, but they seem awfully afraid of something they don't think exists, huh? I have a theory. They believe in ghosts, all right, but they think they're some evil, anti-Christian force."

"It's just a theory," Alvarez reiterated, "and what does it matter? *I* don't care about ending CPM's reign of terror. I just want to go home to my girl and my dog. You'd best do the same," he added sharply, glancing my way. "I've given up on these two." I fixed my eyes back onto Palace, willing her to explain.

She sighed. "I've been here over a year. It means technically, I could graduate from the program if I told them everything they wanted to hear. Too bad. I'm not going to. It wouldn't be right, and *someone's* got to keep protesting things here." Palace's eyes flickered at the rest of us in silent accusation. "If, goddess forbid, this place still stands when I'm eighteen, they can't hold me anyway. Twenty more months." She knocked on the table, though it was metal, not wood.

I stared at Jenika for a second, who had gone back to picking at her sandwich. She seemed to have spread around more of it than she had actually eaten. "What about you?" I prompted.

She shook her head sadly. "I'm not leaving without Petie." Jenika glanced into my eyes, then directed her attention back to her plate. "He needs me here."

In the silence that followed, everyone, even Palace, was subdued. I knew better than to follow the topic. Backtracking a bit, I turned to Palace and, hoping the others no longer expected me to be subtle, asked, "So...you're not dating your ghost-friend, but you do have a girlfriend?"

"Nope. I'm single, and straight...but not narrow." Palace winked, and my face grew hot, though I had always thought that was a silly line.

"But, you said..."

"They think I'm a lesbian, yes." Palace pulled out a spoon from goodness knew where and poked at the bread of her remaining half-sandwich. "Like I said, my friend's a girl, so they think we must have been screwing. Plus, they're always asking about my orientation."

"And she responds with, 'That's none of your damn business, you homophobes,'" Alvarez piped in helpfully.

"Well, what? It's not. As a result, I get the 'don't like girls' treatment as well as the 'don't talk to ghosts.'"

"Oh, Palace." My heart broke just a little bit more. "I can't speak for the whole gay community, but you don't have to suffer for our sakes. I wouldn't be offended if you told them you're straight."

She laid her spoon down with a clink, the sandwich remnants reduced to mush, and folded her arms. "It's okay. More ammunition to seal their fates when they finally get busted for child abuse."

AFTER BRUNCH, I followed Palace back to her room to keep talking. She did not seem to mind, which I suppose is understandable considering how little company she typically had, and the total lack of company she hadn't told her stories before.

Palace had grown up in South Africa and gone on to attend a private boarding school on the East Coast. Her ghost-friend had been inhabiting her dorm room, but no one else, even Palace's roommate, could see her. Soon, Palace's apparent talking to walls had attracted attention, and the headmistress had had Palace hypnotized by a specialist.

Her story gave me the creeps, but she was calm telling me. Maybe it helped that she'd had two years to get used to the idea, or perhaps it was just because Palace could not remember what had happened with the hypnotist. Clearly, she had told him enough of the truth to damn herself to Chose People. Palace missed her younger sister but claimed she had nothing nice to say about her other family members or former friends.

Eventually, our conversation worked around to the other prisoners. It was obvious that, however they may bicker, Palace deeply cared about them. Finally, I screwed up my courage, more afraid of the answer than Palace's possible anger, and asked, "What's going on with Peter?" Confirming my fear of sordidness, she sighed elaborately.

"He can talk, if that's what you mean. He just doesn't, and I can't blame him. He shouldn't be here. I mean, none of us *should*, but...he's only five. He told his parents about his friend who lived in the park, and they saw him holding hands with the air. None of us know if Pete's friend was even a ghost, or just imaginary. His parents have come here twice. From what I gather, mental illness isn't even the point." Palace had fire in her eyes. "They just hate that their son thought about holding hands with a guy."

I shivered. "That's horrible. And it's not like kids holding hands means anything, anyway."

"And so what if it did?" She was right.

We were both quiet for some time. "So, he gets shocks, like I did today?"

"Twice a week, I think," Palace whispered after a moment.

"You 'think'?"

She spoke in a monotone, but her eyes betrayed her emotion. "If you're gonna get shocked, they give you less food. So, there's less on his plate sometimes, but that's the only clue. Everyone else screams sometimes, when a shock's really bad, but Peter doesn't. Not ever."

I struggled to think of a new topic. Failing, I absently glanced at my watch, one of the few personal items I still possessed. Remembering the warning I had received, I made my exit.

# Chapter Thirteen

I LEARNED NOT to defy CPM's curfews, arbitrary as they sometimes seemed. The punishment for failure to meet deadlines or stay sufficiently quiet during meals was a set of spankings, administered by ruler by Ma'am herself. No one in a position of power referred to them as "spankings," though that's what they were; the euphemism of choice was "Punishment Time."

My debut session occurred on the same first full day, after supper and teeth-brushing and before they sent us to bed. I still had to atone for my obstinate behavior upon arrival, Ma'am said. I couldn't tell her about the decision I had made since then, to withdraw inside myself until this interlude ended. In fact, neither of us said anything until ten lashes later, with Ma'am's clipped "You may leave."

I realized my hands were shaking as I walked down the brightly lit hall toward my room. The fact of the spankings startled me, even after everything else.

Passing the open bathroom doorway, I met Jenika's eyes. She paused at the sink, considered me, and seemed to make a decision. Stepping closer, she spoke in a low voice. "It's because your bottom doesn't show marks," she said primly. "And even if it does, we're not going to, you know...if our parents visit." She glanced to either side and then walked past me without another word, as if sharing this information had taken a lot out of her.

I mulled Jenika's conclusion over as I changed into the thin, primrose-colored flannel pajamas laid out on my new bed. True, I had no marks, not that I had expected them through my hardy underwear and gray linen skirt. I still wasn't convinced Jenika was right. Surely Ma'am considered pragmatic things like evidence, but that wasn't the point of spanking us. Nor was the pain, which was mild in comparison to their experiments with electricity.

It was about humiliation, control.

Aside from Punishment Time, which only Palace received more than occasionally, Ma'am never made an appearance at the compound, leaving her henchmen to carry out orders like some sort of minor deity. How funny, in a sad way, that someone so devoutly religious should have a God complex.

My daily schedule began with either what we called "little shocks" or "big shocks"; the latter were what I had experienced my first morning. Palace had not been mistaken: When I asked Dr. Salamander why we and Peter were called in for them twice a week instead of twice a month, he admitted outright the three of us had a special focus since we were "in danger of homosexuality."

Rather than a uniform treatment of big and little shocks all against interaction with ghosts, our amped up plan divided the bigs and littles into exclusively ghost- and gay-related topics, respectively. I wondered if keeping the bigs for the ghostly treatment allowed the employees to disguise what they were *really* concerned about, as well as leaving more time to deal with the homosexuality angle.

I persevered, just as I had resolved to myself I would. The littles, after all, were not too bad. They were only several times as intense as the electric shocks I had sometimes gotten from touching monkey bars or car door handles. Besides, the pain generally stayed in the limb to which it was applied instead of filling my body as the bigs did.

Sometimes, the shock sessions focused exclusively on trying to hardwire me for responses to certain words and, presumably, ideas. For the bigs' ghost-related sessions, the phrases ranged from the obvious, such as *spirit*, to the revealingly irrelevant, such as *Satan* and *incubus*. The anti-gay littles employed predictable words, from *lesbian* to *labia*. Hearing the mildly provocative names of body parts, along with terms like *cunnilingus,* from the mouth of Dr. Salamander made me bite back laughter. I was not able to hold it in when, after a month of only verbal cues, he showed me the first ghost-related image: an old painting of a wispy, see-through woman in a Victorian dress, grinning deviously.

Before I could calm myself, the doctor hit the lever, and laughs turned into chokes as my body went into a spasm. My mind went blank and my limbs filled with pins and needles, but my least favorite part was the sense of having lost all power. After that incident, they did not attempt images for my bigs for the rest of the first half of the year.

I admit I perversely looked forward to the queercentric littles' images. After all, I wondered, will they show pornography? Six months' worth of sessions did not, in fact, provide me with any X-rated images. The most scandalous among them involved bikinis and women kissing one another, and despite their ultimate goal, Sapphic concepts did not become unappealing to me. Recalling specific images that had accompanied shocks made me feel uneasy, but that was as much of a mental impact as Dr. Salamander managed to impart on my fantasies.

Several of the guards—from what I could tell, there were about a dozen—including my least favorite advised me against spending time with Palace. They viewed her as a bad influence, but ultimately, they could not keep us from talking at the table, even when our days were kept full of appointments. Like the ban on outside media, policy officially encouraged patients to converse to "focus on their recovery."

My favorite parts of the day, of course, were meals, one of which usually occurred after our morning shock sessions and the other after the sun had set. The other kids were often moody, prone to argue passionately about silly things or to temporarily join Peter as silent observers, but their company was still a luxury. Later, I realized each of us trapped in CPM had showed glimpses of the damage with which we would grapple for the rest of our lives. Still, it's hardly an exaggeration to say the comfort I derived from them was my lifeblood.

I can barely remember enjoying the actual food at our mealtimes, though. Aside from the fruit, most everything we were served tasted gelatinous.

Otherwise, our only organized activities were Bible Time after dinner and counseling in midafternoon. At other hours, we were directed toward the personalized sets of workbooks which allowed CPM to call itself a school. Mine included Geometry, US History, and a collection of short writings followed by multiple choice questions. Nothing proved difficult enough to keep me occupied for long.

I sometimes wondered if our porous schedule was a strategic move, designed to make us shape up and earn our privilege to wander in the sunny outside square in the center of the building. Although feeling sunlight that didn't come through a barred window sounded nice, I shuddered at the idea of enduring pat-downs before coming back inside. Being at the beginning of the program at least saved me from that indignity.

As for Bible Time, despite being hungry for reading material, I generally only pretended to participate. I had read the entire Bible at a young age and had long since gleaned any joy I could from its stories. Besides, the copies the guards gave us were soft-backed for protection, and though I had never met her, this made me think of Daze and her weaponized hardcover.

Inevitably, this led to my painful missing of Gem. At first, I tried to keep my feelings at bay. I would not hear my love's voice again until I earned the privilege of receiving phone calls, and even that would be difficult for Gem to navigate and impossible for us to plan. The best thing I could do just then, I decided, was to fake the evolution they wanted and get out as soon as possible. If the mandatory minimum was one year, I'd be away from Gem for one year, and not a day longer. I would say what they wanted to hear, in disconnected empty words, with smiles affected at will.

While I could not have predicted it, I liked my counseling sessions even less than the bigs. My first session with Nanette—the only CPM worker to use her first name, probably to encourage a sense of closeness— consisted of me reiterating the story of how I had come to be there. I knew better than to lie then, since Ma'am had given her my basic history in notes, anyway.

However, by our second session I was ensconced in a plan: to stage my own transformation into a liver of definitive religion, heterosexuality, and ghost-free existence. This required me to go along with trains of thought I found ludicrous and, more often than not, insulting.

"Why do you think you find women attractive?"

"Well, I—I don't know."

"How is your relationship with your mother?"

"We're not close."

"So maybe you were seeking a mother figure!" Nanette cried triumphantly, as if she had solved a logic puzzle no one else had managed.

I seethed inside and decided I couldn't resist putting up at least a bit of a visible fight. "I'm not any closer to my father, though…"

"Ah." She nodded and opened her eyes wide. "Do you think he scared you off from men, then?"


WE CELEBRATED MY fifteenth birthday in the established CPM manner: the staff members did not mention it and the fellow inmates treated me with the usual song and a cluster of hugs at dinner. The others joked about giving me their food, which, while it was the most appealing gift they had, was of course not appealing at all.

When Palace's birthday rolled around, we would make the same jokes and not acknowledge their previous use. Still, the simple token of their camaraderie warmed me, and, more than ever, I appreciated not being alone in this troubling milieu.

In some ways, I came to feel being at CPM was actually better than life at my parents' house. The littles and bigs were bad, but at least I knew when they would happen. I had never known when my parents would go off, and the terror of knowing it could happen at any time had been worse than the hitting itself. The rare Punishment Time was at least silent, in contrast to my father's verbal attacks. I knew, after all, what the staffers at CPM wanted to hear, and I had never been sure with my mother and father. Until the moment with Leigh and the knife, they had thought I was living just as they wanted—good grades, not too social, supposedly Christian—but they had still always found reasons to rage at me.

My parents' house had Gem, though. She overrode everything. Sure, sometimes I missed the sex, but that was the least of it. My body ached to be held at night, and my mind short-circuited without our long conversations.

Then again, my brain stayed half-asleep on the best of days—foggy with inertia, fuzzy with electricity. Sometimes I found myself at a meal with no memory of having walked there, or opened a workbook to finished pages I did not recall filling out. *This is good*, I told myself. *It means time is passing.*

I had not yet been awarded the privilege of receiving phone calls, so I did not hear from my parents. This relieved me, seeing as I had no desire to speak with them and did not want to extend my "reformed former ghost-dater" act to them yet. Still, I couldn't help daydreaming up scenarios in which they called and then were both drawn away from the phone, allowing Gem to pick up the receiver for a quick declaration of love. *Soon enough,* I told myself, *I'll be with her again.*

DURING MY FOURTH month, Alvarez completed his program. Despite his assurance, identical to mine and Palace's, that CPM's philosophy was bullshit, he had clocked in at a year and passed their verbal tests of conversion with flying colors. Our goodbyes were bittersweet, and even Peter, in the first words I'd ever heard him speak, accompanied his hug with a tearful "I miss you."

The entire twelve-pack of guards came out to restrain us for the occurrence of a landmark I had never before seen a patient reach: an exit through an outside door. Opposite the part of the circle in which we had our room, and directly across from Dr. Salamander's office, one guard paused in manhandling us to undo a complex series of locks, finally running his ID card through a slot in the wall to make the door open.

It seemed impossibly bright outside as Alvarez stepped out with a giant smile, even thinking to turn and wave at us as he walked toward Ma'am's van, on his way to his dog, his ghostly girlfriend, and a family to whom he would lie for the rest of his life.


DESPITE MY JEALOUSY, I was genuinely happy for Alvarez. After all, he had accomplished exactly what I intended to do with a similar mindset. Better yet, Peter's year would be over in two more months, and then Jenika would stop pretending she needed more time and depart as well. Though I barely knew them, particularly Jenika, who seemed to retreat into herself even while talking, I would miss them too. Still, any encouragement in this dismal environment would be welcome.

Later that week, Palace's shouts carried down the hall. I had never known her to be so loud. She would have a spanking session with Ma'am come night, without a doubt. I hurried to her room, hoping to quiet her before I could be caught outside my own bedroom after curfew, and stopped short at the sight of Jenika, paler than usual, huddled on her bed. "What's going on?"

Palace sidled up next to me, arms folded. "Tell her what you just told me," she commanded Jenika.

"Uh—I said...maybe I actually *am* ill. I mean, maybe my boyfriend was a hallucination." Jenika pulled her knees up under her chin, squinted at the floor, and in a whisper, repeated the line I knew had caused Palace's scream in the first place. "Maybe ghosts don't exist after all."

Palace spun toward me. "What are we going to do with her? Wasn't anyone watching when she drank the Kool-Aid?"

"Palace," Jenika whimpered, "don't yell at me. I'm just trying to figure this out. If our ghosts are all real, why can't everybody see them?"

"No one knows why," I spoke up. "Only certain people see certain ghosts, and a lot of them can't see each other, either. I bet, actually, a lot more people see them than we think. Most probably never tell anyone, and some don't even know the ghosts *are* ghosts, I'm sure." Palace sighed and began to unclench her arms.

"But the thing is," Jenika pressed, "I believe in God."

"So do I; so what?" Palace demanded.

I turned to her in surprise. "You do?"

She raised an eyebrow. "She loves the cynics too, Cassie." I hid my smile.

"Palace, if you believe in God, why do you say 'she'?" Jenika groaned.

"Why don't you? I'm assuming God has no gender, so isn't 'he' just as weird?"

"Okay, fine," conceded Jenika. "Anyway, though, don't ghosts seem against belief in God?"

"Why? Even if you just go by the Bible, can you tell me where it says spirits never have to stick around on Earth a while? Maybe they have unfinished business...or maybe Earth is the Catholic purgatory."

Jenika appeared to be thinking hard. "Hmm." After a while, she spoke again. "I've always felt like an outcast. Like there was something different about me. Even if your ghosts are both real, who's to say there's not something wrong with *me*?"

Palace let out another of her signature crisp, short sighs. "Fine, Jenika. Let's say, for the sake of a very fucking stupid argument, that there *is* something wrong with your brain. Shouldn't you be in a real mental hospital, then, instead of this screwy ex-ghost camp? If that's what you decide you need, even then you have to get out of here first."

Jenika stood up off the bed. "I guess you're right."

"I know I am." Palace's voice softened. "Listen," she said, laying a hand on Jenika's shoulder, "I appreciate you staying around to keep a special eye on Peter. I really do, and I know he does too, even if they've messed him up too badly to tell you so. But you've paid your dues, Jenika. You need to get out of here and live your life." Wiping away a stray tear, Jenika hurried back toward her bedroom.

Realizing I had barely spoken, or wanted to, since I had stepped in, I turned to Palace. "That's nice of you to say. I think what *you're* doing, though—staying here to show them they can't break everyone—is really important too."

She shrugged and turned her head away, not appearing proud at all. "Sure. And if I got out, where would I go?" Palace's eyes were suspiciously shiny. "I don't have the motivators you all do."

"But even if you can't get back to your friend," I pushed, wondering if I should leave her alone, "there's your family..." She shook her head emphatically.

"I'm not going back there. Believe it or not, this is better."

A chill ran over my arms. "What do you mean?" I whispered, already knowing I would regret the question.

"My stepmom shipped me to boarding school because she had, as she says, 'had enough of my sick accusations.' I had spoken the truth, though, about...what she was referencing. But she told everyone I made it up, including the people here when I first arrived. Let me guess: Nanette tried to find reasons you would hate your father, right?" I nodded. "Well, with me they're pretty easy to pinpoint."

An awful silence hung in the air between us, a quiet that went on too long to mean anything but what I feared it meant. "Oh, Palace. No."

"Yep." Her eyes flickered between vulnerability and hard resignation.

I wanted to tell her about Mackey's puffy hands, maybe even about the pair of kids who had drugged Gem, but I doubted hearing of more sorrow and violation would help her. Instead, I just gave Palace a hug fraught with meaning: free of the eroticism of my hugs with Gem, but far more intimate than anything I had ever shared with my school friends. She returned the gesture gently at first, then her arms tightened around me, more close and urgent contact than I had experienced since before my fight with Leigh. I had never before been someone's life preserver.

"What the hell is this?" We broke apart. Two guards, including the especially awful one, stood before us, lips curled in derision and triumph.

*Oh, well,* I thought, as they led me back to my room. *I'll just pile on the contrition later. I can handle a few spankings.*

THAT NIGHT, PALACE woke me with a hand on my shoulder. "Can I stay with you for a while?"

I'll admit I wondered if she intended anything sexual. People made jokes, after all, about straight men messing around in jail. It disturbed me to realize I might not even say no—I still loved Gem, but I trusted Palace and was so, so lonely.

When she climbed into my bed, though, I knew this was still just about comfort. We kept a space between us and didn't cuddle, but she took my hand. My body buzzed at Palace's touch; I had been starved of physical contact, like an empty battery.

"Gem was in a place like this," I whispered. "She got through it. We will too."

"Your girl?" she whispered back. I nodded, and even though she couldn't see my head, she could sense the movement.

"The more things fuckin' change—" Palace began, but she started sobbing before she could finish the sentence. Her sobs were hard but quiet, and apparently the guards didn't hear her, because we remained undisturbed.

We squeezed each other's hands until her tears stopped. With a breathed "Thanks," she stood and tiptoed back to her room.

# Chapter Fourteen

AS PLANNED, PETER graduated from the program in December, at which point Jenika pretended to have a sudden breakthrough. Though she had been insisting she was not ready to leave CPM since her year had run up, she now agreed it was time. If any of the staffers found this fishy, they said nothing of it. Maybe even they were not evil enough to deny two scared, lonely kids a few more months of each other's company.

My goodbye with Jenika played similarly to the scenario with Alvarez, but I choked up when it came time to wish Peter off. The unsettling little boy had never spoken a word to me. While he would now be free from the specific brand of agony within those walls, I had no idea to what he was returning, aside from parents deathly afraid of queerness.

While hugging him, I leaned over impulsively and whispered, "Love whomever you want," directly into his ear. It was a risk, considering how many staff members were around, and if I had thought about it beforehand, I wouldn't have done it. Luckily, the guards were preoccupied with making sure the rest of us didn't get too near to the door. Peter drew back and gawked at me, startled, with wide, red-rimmed eyes. I hoped he would remember my words and, at some point, find people or therapy to mitigate the effects of what had happened to him.

Apparently no new kids with religious parents had revealed ghostly friendships this season. Palace and I were alone together within the ring. This did not alter the dealings of my daily life too much, seeing as I had rarely spoken to the other prisoners anyway, but the relative lack of footsteps in the hall proved eerie. I wished in vain for some sort of updates from each of them, but I had to assume hearing nothing was a good sign.

The coming of Christmas meant little to us at CPM. If I had not been marking each day on a scrap of paper with felt-tip markers, our sole approved writing utensils, I would not even have known when a new month began, let alone a major holiday. Dr. Salamander, however, did pass the word along from Ma'am that we were to spend Christmas Day reading the Bible only, and all our appointments would be cancelled. Apparently, everyone would have Christmas off but us and a small handful of guards.

More auspicious than the holiday season, however, was my sixth month mark. Since I had behaved as expected, said I was desperate to change, I would be given "receiving phone" and "outdoors" privileges. There would also be a newly arranged schedule, but that part was irrelevant to me. The so-called "outdoors privileges" barely mattered either, as I had already resolved not to wander into the donut unless utterly desperate for sunlight. I wanted to give the guards as few excuses to pat me down as possible. They were only cruel, not sleazy, but I still didn't like the idea of strange men being sanctioned to touch me. No, the ability to receive phone calls was the only new one I cared about.

When my six-month anniversary arrived, though, I found plenty else to distract me. My early visit to Dr.

Salamander held a particularly nasty surprise. While I sat in the chair and waited expectantly, he situated himself in the middle of the room, fingers steepled as if addressing a congregation.

"Today," he began, "we will not be dealing with your latent hallucinations. Our severe shock sessions will center around further undoing your homosexual tendencies, with minor shock sessions for the paranormal issues. We want to finish your treatment with absolute assurance you will not revert to that godless lifestyle, which seems to be more prevalent in our world right now than consorting with spirits."

"What?" I protested, but already, I kicked myself for having been so naïve. For all my theorizing about why conditioning against homosexuality lay only with the littles, I had never guessed my treatment was on a simple half/half plan. Dr. Salamander repeated himself stiffly, and I reminded myself this couldn't be much worse than the previous arrangement. "I mean, that's okay, I guess. I just wasn't expecting it."

Dr. Salamander raised an eyebrow but said nothing. Instead, he flipped on the projector and the session's first photo blinked into focus: a butch/femme couple walking on a sidewalk, hand in hand. My mind went blank as he hit the switch and I began to spasm. *How horrible*, I imagined saying bitterly when the shakes in my body began to subside; *a loving couple*. My insides boiled with rage at the doctor and his colleagues.

The obligatory bikini photos passed, followed by, at long last, soft pornography. I stared, immediately received punishment for doing so, and began the process over again. These were the first genuinely risqué images I had seen in a year, since two days before my math final when I lay with my girlfriend's genuine, tangible body. I wanted to bring my eyes out of focus to fight against the process, but I found I couldn't. I was starved for sexual stimulation and more responsive to the pictures than I had previously ever been to erotica.

As pain wracked me like a rag doll, I would have given anything just to have a minute alone with the photos, a minute when I could enjoy what I desired without being simultaneously condemned for it. As usual, the doctor screamed at me if I tried to close my eyes, and for the first time I worried the agony I underwent at CPM would follow me back into my regular life in flashbacks.

Then a voice, faint beyond the crackle of electricity, warbled, "One more..."

A picture flipped onto the projection screen of a fully clothed, innocent-looking girl, smiling as if for a school picture. I inhaled sharply, falling into a coughing fit.

It was Gem. *My* Gem. She was younger and dressed differently than I had ever seen, but it was unmistakably her. "No!" I screamed and had the sensation of my heart exploding as I went into another full-body tremor.

When it left me still and panting, Dr. Salamander stood and asked, "The verdict?"

"It's definitely the right girl." I opened my eyes. Ma'am sat in a folding chair on my other side, grinning in triumph. I had not heard her come in, but then I'd had plenty to distract me. "It's the one she hallucinated, all right." Ma'am turned to me without altering her smile. "She was so hard to find, Cassandra. You never gave us a last name, but between your address and the city of Baton Rouge's reform school records, we had a stroke of luck. I had been starting to think Gem came totally from your imagination, but the delusions are usually figures from history."

I knew, logically, that to keep my act up I should probably thank them for finding a way to make my treatment more intense, but I would sooner bite off my own tongue. Instead, I slumped over in the chair with my eyes shut, feigning exhaustion. I had once passed out after a set of bigs, after all. I wished I could make myself do so now.

Ma'am's voice grew fainter. "Have them take her to her room when she comes to. She can miss a meal, seeing as she'll probably be nauseous anyway."

I waited several long minutes, made a disoriented-seeming show of waking up, and let myself be led, eyes straight ahead, to my bedroom. They gave me the rest of the morning to sob in peace.

I WANTED TO stay in bed past the time for my counseling session, but if I did, I would be subjected to a set of spankings, and I could not face Ma'am again so soon. When the time came, I stumbled down the hall, my face red and salty with unwiped tears and my hair tangled and matted, past Palace's worried stare, to the opposite side of the donut. Nanette raised an eyebrow at me but struck me as excited, for some reason, when I sat down. Perhaps she enjoyed my lack of dignity. "You seem upset," Nanette opened with a grin, confirming my suspicion of morbid pleasure.

"I had a hard session of bigs this morning—big shocks."

She nodded. "I know what 'bigs' are, Cassandra. I'm in touch with the slang here." A smirk approached my face, and I tried to think it away. "So, what made today's round so difficult?"

I could lie, but what would be the point? I knew Nanette was in touch with Ma'am and Dr. Salamander anyway and more than likely already knew about their mid-year surprise. "They found a picture of the girl I thought I knew as a ghost. She was a real person, it turns out, and they put her photo at the end of the slides."

"Ahhh," she intoned in a long breath, sifting through her papers. "And today, you moved to big shocks for homosexuality and littles for ghost tendencies, if I'm not mistaken."

I had a sudden fantasy about bolting up and strangling Nanette from the other side of the desk, which made me disgusted with myself. Despite what everyone must have assumed, I did not believe I was a violent person.

"That's right." I gritted my teeth a bit and pushed on. "The doctor explained, and I understand why they're doing it. The picture, though, really startled me." She nodded in an illusion of sympathy. "I guess it's because...I've come to accept Gem wasn't real. Seeing an image of her, even if it's from decades ago, gave me a fright, especially since they shocked me at the same time."

I listened to the bullshit I was spouting, and, while I still hated CPM with all my might, I felt a wave of shame for myself. After all, I had caused such a nuisance in the mainstream world they had relegated me here, to huge psychological warfare. I knew what Palace would say, because she had before: CPM was only supported by obscure fringe groups, deceived families about what really went on, and did not act in accordance with child treatment laws. Yet in the eyes of much of the world, I deserved this. I struggled to not hate myself sometimes...*but I'm halfway through,* I remembered. *I can do this without letting them break me.*

Nanette was drying up a long stream of pious lecture. "And knowing how very unhappy you've made God with your occult fanaticism and your self-declared desire to lie with other women, it's perfectly natural to feel ashamed and shocked at an image representing the sinful things you've done."

I nodded, angry with myself for again nearing the self-hating vulnerability on which they depended. I stayed silent and agreed to every religious platitude Nanette lobbed at me before biting my lip, tucking my hair behind my ears, and trotting off to dinner.

AS WE ATE, Palace eyed me but did not comment on my disheveled appearance. I did not kid myself about it being noticeable, seeing as how I had earned a reputation, even when there were only five of us, for taking the most care with my looks. This seemed hilarious, when I stopped and thought about it, given how little attention people thought I paid in the outside world.

Neither of us spoke until a guard hulked up. This caught our attention right away, considering they seemed to view the patients' dining area as a type of ghetto. "You have a phone call," he announced, square jaw barely moving.

In the quagmire of the day, I had forgotten the reason I'd wanted it to come.

The guard led me to a small door near Dr. Salamander's shock room and began to work on its complicated series of locks. It opened onto a room hardly larger than an old-fashioned telephone booth, with a retro pink plastic apparatus attached to the wall to match. I picked up the receiver, which dangled toward the floor, bouncing against the soft wall, and whispered, "Hello?"

"Hello, darling." My heart sank; it was only Mother and, worse yet, she was crying. "It's so good to hear your voice. Your father and I have missed you so much!"

I sighed. Of course she claimed to miss me; others would expect as much. Maybe she missed someone, but it wasn't me. It was the ideal image of a daughter she projected onto me, telling herself I would become what she wanted if she just pushed harder.

I wondered what she had been telling people about why I had been taken away. I had a hunch it involved a rare disease, and an all-but-certainty it had nothing to do with getting in a fight at school. If she had wanted to be the object of pity for the church, the word *homosexuality* might have come up, but I doubted it. All the adults with power over my life seemed convinced my sexual orientation had something to do with her. She wouldn't want to come off badly.

"Hi, Mother. I'm doing well here. I've made friends. I'm getting better." I turned behind me toward the doorway, and sure enough, there stood the guard; my new privilege did not include privacy. I wrapped up the conversation as hastily as I could without making it my obvious intention. Still, I had to exchange a few words with Father. Our sentences were so terse they seemed to cut me with their awkwardness, until I finally hung up to head back for the dining box. Surprising me, the guard closed himself into the phone room. *Is he on hours of constant telephone duty?* I wondered. For just a second, I felt sorry for him.

When I sat back down to my cold, gummy pork chops, Palace gaped at me. "I got call-receiving privileges today," I muttered with a stab of guilt. Palace, of course, had never received any such thing, because she continued to bravely rock the boat and speak her mind while I succumbed and pretended.

No sooner had I begun to think about this than the same disgruntled guard approached. "Someone's calling you *again*," he complained. Well, they didn't pay him to hide his annoyance.

I trudged back down the hall, wondering what obnoxious detail about the minor characters in my former life Mother had forgotten. "Hello?"

There was a pause, and then: "Hi."

"Hi!" I startled at the sound of her voice. My heart tightened with love, radiating tingles through my chest. I had never needed communication with her more than I did today. "Oh, Ge-Janice," I caught myself just in time, sneaking a glance at the guard. Maybe he would not have recognized my ghost's name, but I could not take the risk. "It's so good to hear from you."

"You too." I could tell Gem was crying too, but from her it didn't seem disingenuous. "I'm sorry it's so late in the day; your folks only just now left the house. Your mother put the number in her purse before she left, but I saw her dial, so...God, what am I talking about? Cassie, I miss you. I want you here."

Relief flooded me. While it had never seemed rational, I'd had a niggling fear for months that Gem would stop loving me. "I miss you too, Janice. Very much."

Gem stayed silent for a moment, putting together the situation. "Someone's listening to you?"

"Yes."

"Can they hear *me*?"

"I don't think so." If they had, someone would have wrestled the phone from me by now, but I could think of no way to tell her this under the circumstances.

"Love, it took me forever to figure out what had happened to you. I'm still not sure I understand where you are."

"It's pretty weird," I confirmed. "I'll explain everything once I get back...which should be in exactly six months!"

"I'll count the days! Cassie," Gem began, her voice getting low and serious, "what's it like there? I mean...is it bad?"

"Yes," I whispered. I heard her sniffle. "I'm okay, though. I have friends—well, one friend."

"I wish there were something I could do to help you."

"Just calling sometimes is enough...and be there to greet me when I return."

"Of course. I can't wait to have my arms around you."

I closed my eyes. "Sounds great." She spoke loving words to me for a while, which I was frustrated not to be able to return in kind. Obviously, it was nice nonetheless, so much nicer than anything I had been able to have in CPM over these long months.

Finally, the guard coughed and tapped his watch. "Your time is up," he added, as if I couldn't have figured out what he meant.

"I have to go now," I groaned. "But, Janice! Thank you so much for calling. I love you. You're the best cousin ever." Gem laughed sadly and said her own goodbyes, and I returned once more to my pork chops. Palace had already disappeared to her bedroom.

TWO MONTHS, SIXTEEN shudder-inducing bigs, and eight sneaky calls with Gem later, Palace woke me in the middle of the night. "Get up, Cassie," she hissed. "We need to talk."

I sat up, wiping my eyes. On the nights after bigs, I always slept like the non-ghostly dead. "And it couldn't have waited a few hours?"

"I didn't want to take a chance." Palace hopped on top of the bed and swiveled to face me, sitting pretzel style. "I think I'm going to break out."

Instantly, I was awake. "What?"

"You heard me." I could not remember her ever sounding so agitated. "I can't keep waiting forever. We need to get out and get the media on this place's ass, and now. Between us, if we plan enough, I'm sure we can pull it off."

"But I only have a few more months!" I hissed. "And you'll be eighteen soon after that. We'll be home free."

"I can't wait. I can't keep doing this: getting trashed for telling the truth, walking around with a target on my head for their personal issues, basically being tortured every morning. Then I'm deemed disrespectful of their arbitrary rules and sent to Ma'am so she can get her rocks off hitting me."

I shivered. "You really think she enjoys it?"

"I 'really think' she had a pronoun slip tonight."

"Huh?"

Palace chuckled in spite of her anger. "There she was, pounding away at my butt, raving about how bad a girl I am." I had goose bumps. Ma'am rarely said more than two words to me, and never during Punishment Time. I'd even been grateful for it before. But given my acquiescence, it made sense that Palace would trigger more ire. "So, she segues into how awful consorting with ghosts is, and how she did it herself, so she knows how 'deeply in danger' I am," she narrated, imitating Ma'am's authoritarian voice. "Toward the end, she gets so into it she doesn't notice she just referred to her ghostly boyfriend as *she*."

My head spun. "No. I mean, maybe you misheard? Or it was a mistake. I've said 'her' instead of 'him' before and stuff like that."

She sighed, letting her face fall into her palms. "Even if I'm wrong, can you deny this place is sick?" I couldn't, of course. "You'll help me get out, won't you? If we can get a hold of a news station, I bet someone will even offer us a place to stay."

"Palace. I can't."

"Yes, you can."

"No!" I lowered my voice again. "You know I hate it here too, but there's no way. They'd catch us both, and then we'd be here for ages."

"We would not, and you know it. Like you said, I'm not far from the end of the tunnel. You're worried about yourself, that they'll keep *you* until you're eighteen."

"Well, yeah! No one's going to help me if I don't do it myself. I want to get back to my life, Palace. I doubt escape's possible anyway. Has anyone ever broken out of here?"

"Why would they tell us if someone had? You're just making excuses. I'm starting to think you're just like Alvarez and Jenika. They danced on out and have brought no attention whatsoever to the atrocities here. Doesn't it piss you off?"

"It's not their fault," I protested. "They have their own lives, and I'm sure they just want to forget all this. I understand it. I mean, not everyone can be a hero."

Her silhouette turned toward me for a few moments, then she sprang off the bed and out the door. "I thought you were different," she spat from just outside in the hallway.

MY FRIENDSHIP WITH Palace never recovered. She took to ignoring me, putting on a carefree face while avoiding my eyes when we were in the same box. Life at CPM without her companionship was achingly lonely, but I could think of nothing to make it up to her save agreeing to a half-baked escape plan. I could never risk it.

I took to spending my appointment-free time weeping in my room, aside from the rare occasion both of my parents left the house long enough for Gem to call. At least Dr. Salamander never went for her photo again. Still, the days of the bigs were particularly bad now my treatment focused on trying to create a Pavlovian pain response to lesbian pornography. When I remembered Gem, or pictured being with other girls, I felt fine, but I could not imagine ever seeing dirty pictures again without remembering the shocks.

After several nervous weeks without incident from Palace, I assumed her plan had gone the way of the similar schemes by Gem's boarding school classmates: a fun set of daydreams, but never approaching fruition.

So when I woke to a commotion in the early hours of the morning, ten weeks before my release date, it took me longer than it should have to figure out what was happening.

I jumped through my doorway and raced toward the sounds of the shouting. The noise was dominated by staccato bursts of words in a high voice and long, chaotic shouts in a lower tone. As I rounded the bend of the donut, I slipped and fell, heels over head, onto a floor slick with dark wetness. As time seemed to stop, I realized it was blood; soon after, I realized from where it had come.

My eyes followed the bloody trail to my least favorite guard, on his knees, clutching at something hanging from his eye. The agonized, primal shout came from him.

"I said, shut the fuck up!" yelled Palace, standing at a door fumbling with the set of keys she had taken. I could not imagine how she had figured out which guard among them had the keys; probably, I'll never know.

As she matched keys to locks, my mind worked in slow motion. I don't know if it was the sleep or the adrenaline, although I'd assume adrenaline would do the opposite. When the guards' boots began stampeding behind me, though, I knew she wouldn't make it. The notion of what would happen to her filled me with dread. "Stop!" I shouted, just as a set of hands reached and restrained me, as if I had anywhere to go.

When Palace hustled out the guard's ID card and slid it through the last lock with a flourish, my brain clicked into action. I realized what, even in the world of her apparent plan, was wrong with this picture. "Palace, no!"

But she yanked the door open and charged...directly into a tiny room with nothing but a buttonless phone.

AN HOUR OF screams later, Dr. Salamander successfully treated the guard's lacerations and removed the spoon from his eyeball. Ma'am informed Palace, in an icy, measured voice, that she may have damaged his sight irreparably and the staff members should probably alert the police.

Palace leaned forward, ice for ice, and replied, "And tell them what? And—tell—them—*what*?" Threats lurked in the air between them, and Ma'am changed the subject.

I assumed Palace had used the same spoon she had played with on my very first day. Only she knew where she had hidden it or how she had sharpened the edge.

For lack of a better place to put us, the other three guards, who had witnessed the tail end of the event, had gathered us, Nanette, and a stone-cold Ma'am in the counseling office. I shared the couch with a tied-up and handcuffed Palace, though I faced away once I realized the sight of her helpless made me tear up. I could not let my sympathy for her show in front of them.

The whole scene reminded me of the time I had spent flanked by Leigh and Grace in Ms. Tucker's office, just before I had made my terrible mistake. Like then, reports corroborated to indicate my innocence. Still, as I dragged myself back to my room in CPM-issued pajamas marred by damp blood, this time I felt sorry for the guilty party, sorrier than she could know.

BEFORE MORNING, NOISE broke through my sleep again. I crept to the doorway, and my notion that CPM had ever been safer than my parents' place came crashing down.

The guard, now with an eye patch, held Palace against the wall with a long hand pressed against her throat. Another guard stood behind his colleague without moving. She shoved at the man she had blinded, but he was much bigger than her. My heart hammered. *If he tries to molest her,* I told myself, *I won't let it happen. I can't. I don't care if they keep me here forever.*

I have no doubt Palace feared the same thing, but the guard stuck to non-sexual violence. As Palace began to gag, eyes wide, he punched her in the stomach. She seemed to be choking in a way I didn't understand, until he pushed her to the wall one more time and let go. As he stomped away, she began to vomit on herself. She slid down the wall, coughing up bile until nothing more came out, then panted for a long minute.

The remaining guard continued to lean against the wall, impassive. He had let this happen. I yearned to go to Palace, try to comfort her, but I knew she would not want to see me. I had let it happen too.

I went to bed and lay there, biting my hand to keep from crying out loud. Maybe protecting myself was the only way to get home, but I wasn't making anything better for the other victims here, or the ones who would come after me. Palace challenged the status quo every day. She was a fighter, an activist, a champion. I knew how to hold on to my convictions and lie convincingly, but I was still just a prisoner.

The image of the still guard, just standing there blank-faced, haunted me as much as anything. How many times had he seen such a thing before? I wondered if he would have intervened if his colleague had tried to rape Palace or kill her. In my gut, I knew the answer was no.

I DID NOT see Palace for a number of weeks, because she had been locked in her room, a makeshift solitary confinement. After the lock-in ended, her face had thinned, but since we could not speak, I did not know if they had restricted her food. They no longer allowed Palace to eat at the patients' dining table or spend any time unescorted by staff members, so it was like I was the only child there.

My graduation day from the program arrived without further fireworks. During each phone call, I informed Gem I would have lots to tell her, but with a guard listening, it all had to wait. I did not trust myself to relate the story of Palace's attempted escape and sound impartial.

At least the guard who had taken a sharp spoon to the eye, who had slammed me with *queer* remarks and beaten my friend, was no longer at CPM. We would not ask, and they would not tell, what had become of him.

On my final morning, after my last set of shocks, Dr. Salamander informed me Nanette had asked for a mini-session before my parents were to arrive. *What the hell,* I thought; *might as well check in with as many mad scientists as possible before I leave the lab.* When I arrived, Nanette grinned like a lipsticked clown behind her desk. I had a seat on the sofa, the pattern of which still showed hints of the blood Palace and I had carried in.

"Cassandra, my dear, today you will go back into the frightening world, but I think you will navigate its temptations successfully. You have grown to show true contrition for your former blasphemous ways. Today, I wanted to approach one of my favorite topics, which I also think will provide an uplifting spring in your step as you leave our facility: virginity."

I nearly choked on my own saliva. *One of her favorite topics?*

"It's a controversial subject when it comes to people like you, who strayed so far they imagined sexual relations with a spirit." Nanette proceeded to explain, without a hint of irony. Some, she said, might consider me to be unequivocally a virgin, full stop, since my sexual partner had not truly existed and had also been a girl, "thus disabling actual sex."

However, Nanette cautioned, the issue was more complicated; the Bible considered sinful thought just as damaging as physical sin. "So in God's eyes," Nanette proclaimed, "you did lie with a female ghost, even though that's so silly! You meant to do it, so it's like you did." She explained the concept of "secondary virginity," saying if I were to proclaim my pure intentions to God, I would be as virginal in soul as I technically was in body.

"Let us pray," she finished, as relentlessly cheerful as ever. "Dear Lord, please forgive Cassandra for her terrible fantasies. Help her in her life outside as she combats homosexual temptations and keep her happy enough that her mental illness does not flare up and cause her to hallucinate unholy beings. Amen."

I squinted at Nanette, with her head bowed and her eyes closed. I imagined other people she might have become, superimposed them over the figure in the long wool dress. If she had grown up in a different faith, or even fallen in with a gentler fringe group, would she be any less devout to its cause?

I wondered if anything could make her denounce CPM. I wondered how, if she left, she would justify her life.

I SAVED THE one goodbye I actually cared about for the last five minutes before Ma'am's van arrived.

"Palace?" I inquired softly, standing in her doorway. She turned away from me and, having nothing else to occupy her, stared out the window at nothing. Barely three feet away, her personal day-guard stood at attention just in case she tried anything funny.

"I'm leaving soon. I just wanted to tell you, well...good luck," I tried, hoping she would know what I meant even as it sailed over the guard's head. I wished her luck in exposing Chose People, yes, but also in eventually forgetting them. Plus, I wanted to hold on to the image of her freedom, not of the abuse she might still face before it arrived. "I'll miss you."

She turned her head toward me, just a fraction, and smiled. It was only a little at the corners of her mouth, but it was enough to encourage me.

"Cassandra!" a guard called. "Time's up."

I pulled a square of toilet paper and my felt-tipped pen out of my pocket and scrawled. "And later, if you ever want to know me, you'll know where I am." I laid my address on the bedspread next to her and hurried away, afraid to wait and see if she would read it.

MA'AM DID NOT speak a word to me until we pulled up, at long last, to the house on Dauphine Street. Then, she surprised me by laying a hand on my knee and simply saying, "Congratulations."

The van pulled away in a humid cloud of dark smoke. It felt strange to be in my own clothes, the same outfit I had been taken in the year before. When I judged myself ready, I turned to face my parents, who had already come outside.

"Sweetie," Mother sighed, wrapping me in a smothering hug. "I'm so glad to have you back." When she finally released me, Father weakly echoed the gesture, arms limp. "Is there anything you'd like to do to celebrate? Should we go for ice cream or beignets?"

"No, thanks," I muttered, wondering if we wanted to "celebrate" the same thing. "I'd just like to be alone for a while...to read. I didn't get to read at the center."

"You'll have to tell us all about it!" she insisted, trailing after me toward the house.

I cringed, facing away from them and the fair-haired lost child who had stopped to gape at us from across the street. "Maybe later?"

"Sure, sure. I have to say, though, I've had a great idea for an event to start your new life. Someone's got a sweet sixteenth birthday coming up, after all!"

I stopped in my tracks, mere feet from the door, simmering. I turned to face her. "A sweet sixteen party? You know I haven't been given a personality transplant, right? And who would I invite, exactly, seeing as I just spent a year in child prison?"

Father turned away and went marching down the road, no doubt more to make a point about how intolerable we were than to actually go anywhere. Mother's mouth fell open. She stared into my eyes for a long moment before she spoke.

"If you haven't changed, I can tell the folks at Chose People and have them come back for you, you know," she whispered hoarsely.

I sighed. "I've changed," I insisted, wearily and deliberately vague. "I just need some time by myself. It's been so long with no privacy." I rushed through the front door.

Luckily, Mother didn't follow too closely behind me. As soon as I opened the door to my bedroom, Gem lurched herself into my arms. I closed us in as quietly as possible, and we moved to the bed, holding each other and letting the tears fall freely. "Oh, Gem," I murmured. "I can't believe we're together again."

"I know." Gem laughed a bit and tried to wipe her tears away. "I thought about posing naked on the bed for your entrance, but I know you might not feel up to anything physical. I'd get it."

"I'll be up to it soon enough," I chuckled. "We'd better wait until they're out, though, or at least asleep. The thing is, Gem...we're going to have to be a lot more careful from now on."

"I know." She nodded. "Do you want to talk about what you've been through?"

I FOUND IT difficult to get used to school again, having missed my entire ninth grade year. Luckily, I had always been ahead of my grade level, but state mandates demanded I still fulfill my ninth and tenth grade work simultaneously to continue on schedule. The workbooks CPM had provided translated to more credits than they probably should have, but I still had to sit twice as many finals. As a result, I met with a certified teacher named Dardin, who typically worked with homeschooled children, twice a week. To keep up, I studied later into the night than I ever could have dreamed.

Still, the arrangement was manageable. In fact, I toyed with the idea of also combining my eleventh and twelfth grade years. The collegiate promises of higher education were infinitely more seductive than anything about high school. I wanted to work up to them as soon as possible.

In addition, I now attended public school for the first time. The high school that worked in conjunction with the Academy had disallowed me, and it was just as well. I could have applied and interviewed at more private institutions, but it didn't seem worth the effort. My parents supported this decision, though I suspect it had as much to do with not wanting to explain my story to religious officials as anything else.

While the academics were not as different in quality as I had been led to believe, the change did take some getting used to, especially the variety of clothes. Aesthetically, the other students distracted me, and I was ill-prepared to make decisions on my appearance early in the morning. In the end, I gave up on trying to appear older or "cool" and went for variations on my old faithful summer uniform: T-shirts and shorts or jeans.

One morning the following winter, I ducked into the kitchen for a bite before I began my school day. My father stared at me, long-faced, with the front page of the paper set in front of him. He beckoned to me. "Is this true?"

I stepped close enough to peer at the article.

### "CHOSE PEOPLE" COMPOUND SHUT DOWN

*Religious anti-paranormal group accused of felonies*

*Last night, a confidential team of Louisiana officials declared the mid-state headquarters of Chose People Ministries closed. The group is being investigated for crimes which include physical and psychological child abuse and practicing medicine, psychiatry, and childcare without appropriate licenses.*

*Whistle-blower Palace Govender, who has waived her right to anonymity, claims to have spent over three years prior to her eighteenth birthday virtually imprisoned in Chose People's center, which she says they marketed to parents as a treatment facility for children who have had visions of ghosts. "Basically, if a minor claims to have seen someone they can't prove exists—*

*teenagers with spiritual experiences, toddlers with imaginary friends—their parent can sentence them to a Chose People program, which is a year long at the least," Govender said in her official statement. "They must sleep at the facility and are not allowed any outside contact, including from family members, until they are declared at least halfway through their treatment."*

*So-called "patients" were apparently treated daily with a beta facsimile of electroconvulsive therapy. Leaders provided them with electricity-based stimuli to induce pain along with words or images related to ghosts.*

*Govender also describes the Chose People complex as possessing an unofficial second agenda for students known or suspected not to be heterosexual. Documents and records confirm that plans for children identifying as lesbian, gay, bisexual, or transgender, or simply declining to say, were markedly different and comparatively brutal, adding to the national discussion about the ethics of conversion therapy.*

"She did it!" I exclaimed.

"You knew the girl, I take it?" Father said softly, eyes fixed on the table. "So, this is all true?"

"Didn't you know it already?"

"You never mentioned the...electricity."

This was true, but then, I had stuck to as little information as possible. I stayed silent for no other reason than that I, like I suspected of Jenika and Alvarez, wanted to put CPM behind me. I still had nightmares about it from which I awoke crying, and I experienced a rising panic inside some small rooms. They had failed to damage my relationship with Gem but had certainly succeeded in making me a more nervous person. The most lasting effect, an inability to trust authority, would be subtler.

I shrugged at my father and said nothing.

"Or the...special program," Father pronounced with a grimace.

"Would it have stopped you, if you'd known?" He remained quiet. "I'm going to be late," I announced with barely restrained disgust. I left him and his avoidant stare, feeling more powerful, somehow, than I ever had before.

# PART THREE

# Chapter Fifteen

ON THE DAY of my first college classes, the sky stayed gray like a perpetual 6:00 a.m. A fine mist hung as low as the traffic lights, accompanied by a chill entirely inappropriate for a Southern autumn.

It didn't matter: I saw the spark.

It was the same spark I had noticed three rows down on that muggy July afternoon we had spent cramped into the Tulane amphitheater. The situation had been unpleasant enough to make me reconsider my choice of universities, but ultimately I had no choice at all. I could not leave Gem. The continued cohabitation with my parents was a tough pill to swallow, but I could pay the price for love.

In any case, the college president's long-winded speech had ended at last. Upon hearing the optimistic addresses by the heads of the Mathematics and English departments, I had left my qualms at bay.

Since I had never understood the expectation of rapt attention to a speaker—why look at someone when you only wanted to hear their words?—I had gotten a head start on my necessary people-watching. My eyes had kept returning to the one young woman close by, though, at her dyed hair, red as a crayon or the Tunnel of Love carnival ride I had never been allowed on as a kid. Her eyes weren't just sparkly; they were shrewd, alive. Her surveillance of the scene had read as confident and bemused. I had been drawn to her immediately, even though she intimidated me.

And now, she sat with a cigarette on the steps of Woolf Hall. In the past weekend of freshman orientation, I had fleetingly mistaken red-headed boys for her several times, but this time it was undoubtedly her. Her established personal uniform of tiny sleeveless tops, baggy pants, and boots covered in buckles exuded a certain blasé coolness that pulled me in like a magnet. I had to know this girl.

Instead of hurrying to catch the first bus back to the corner, I continued down the paved pathway toward Woolf. I took a deep breath and pushed myself out of my comfort zone. After all, this was what college was supposed to be about: wading into uncomfortable situations until one turned out better than you expected. Anyway, we were all lost at sea at this point, so I could afford some awkward extra friendliness. "Hi." I extended a hand, which I realized was perhaps overly formal, but by then it was too late. "I'm Cassie."

"Katia," the redhead asserted, fitting her tiny, smooth digits into mine. "Katia Rodriguez." I sat next to her, as casually as I could manage, and she extended her box of cigarettes toward me in offering.

"Oh, no thanks." Katia slipped it back into the oversize pocket over the side of her knee, probably wondering why I sat with her if not to smoke. *Maybe I should take it,* I thought. *My folks lied about everything else. Then again, smoking really is kind of gross.* "So, where are you from?"

She blew a plume of smoke. "Southern California."

"Really? Like, Los Angeles?"

"No, more central. And not nearly as interesting."

"Ah." I remembered the kids I had grown up with who had lived in the suburbs yet told tourists they lived in New Orleans proper. "I'm a local girl myself."

"Yeah?" Katia's dark eyes landed on me; for the first time in our conversation, I had her attention. "How do you like the city?"

"I love it." My own vehemence surprised me. "I mean, I would have liked to get away for college, to try some new place, but New Orleans really has a culture all its own. It's hard to leave."

"So I've heard." Katia stamped out her cigarette, though from my limited knowledge, it wasn't nearly finished. "Are you a freshman too?"

"Yeah, I finished high school early. I'm eighteen, though," I added, unsure why. The corners of Katia's lips lifted a bit during the short silence.

"Sorry to be rude, but I have to head to work. It's opening weekend and all."

"You work on campus, then?"

"Yep, for the dining hall. Glamorous, eh? Too bad my tuition won't pay itself." We exchanged a smile. Sure, I was glad to not be in her boots, but I couldn't help but feel a little jealous of her independence. To my knowledge, I did not know anyone else paying their own way through a college at which they were boarding. Then again, financial problems or monetary differences between families, let alone anything approaching poverty, had remained an untouchable topic throughout my school years, even when it seemed like an elephant in the room.

Katia and I nodded goodbye, and within seconds, she had power-walked out of sight. Looking at the place where she had been, my insides were warm, despite the sky's threat to lay a minor monsoon on me at any minute. I repeated my awkward words in my head, fine-tuning them until they were sophisticated and bemoaning the versions Katia had heard. Then again, I knew there would be more opportunities for us to talk.

Occasionally, I had an instant connection with strangers and felt they should be in my life. In the past, even when those feelings hadn't panned out into anything meaningful, I had never stopped feeling like they should have.

I impulsively headed for the streetcar, though the buses would get me home sooner. New home or no, I had earned my freedom. Leaning out of the window, I let the fragrant, unpretentious, somehow fresh air hit my face. This must be the heady thrill of having just begun college. For some time, I repeated words in my head like a mantra: *Katia and I will be friends.*

In hindsight, some part of me must have known something was at play besides my social loneliness. I can't pretend I didn't know what I was doing on some deep level, what I was entering into even as I sat there. I suppose it just seemed inevitable.

MOTHER WASTED NO time in shattering my delusions of liberation. She pressed me for details on what we had been taught in my new Advanced Calculus and Biology courses. Unsurprisingly, I had little to tell, it being the first day for both, so finally I handed her the syllabi. I knew it may provoke her to ask endless, more detailed questions as time went on, but I was too exhausted to stay in the kitchen with her.

I closed my bedroom door and greeted Gem, who had been napping on my bed. Even four years after I had first observed the process, the way she could wake fully and instantly, without any between states, was a marvel. "Hey, love. How'd it go?"

"Great." I leaned over for my greeting kiss. "I mean, the classes today were sort of boring, but I feel accomplished to have made this step, if that makes sense. There's something gratifying about just knowing I'm in college now. It feels different, you know?"

Gem shrugged. "I don't *know*, but I can imagine. It's good to hear."

"Thanks." I stopped, realizing how wistful she must feel, witnessing my excitement over college. What could I do, though? We shared everything, and I wouldn't start putting a harness on inconvenient feelings now, especially when they were positive.

"So...new books?" she inquired, breaking into my reverie. Once she helped me out of my giant new backpack, Gem pulled the largest compartment's zipper and surveyed the inside contents.

"Not unless you're interested in the lives of integers."

She rolled her eyes. "Give it a few more months, and I might be." Flopping back onto the bed, Gem nodded at my bookcase. "I mean, darling, you've got impeccable taste, but I practically know everything here by heart."

"I know." I sighed. "I'll get to the library this weekend. I promise. With a whole building of books I haven't seen yet, there's got to be something."

"Sounds good." Gem paused. "You probably need the room to study, huh?"

I rolled my eyes. "Signs point to yes."

"I understand, college girl." Gem touched my hips on her way out and trailed her tongue across my neck, never breaking stride. "No distractions here." I spun around and kissed her hard, as we had both known I would, before she ducked out with that smile I knew so well.

# Chapter Sixteen

BY THE TIME I finished the week, I had shared four short talks and one cafeteria lunch with Katia.

Like Calculus and Bio, my first week's worth of Freshmen English failed to stimulate me. When I entered my last class, though, Women's Studies 101, which I had essentially picked at random, I knew it would be different even before the familiar bright head. Not only was the class much smaller than any lectures I had sat through that week; there were bookcases wall to wall and filled to the brim, many times more books than there were in my English room.

And then the professor began speaking. Loud, hilarious, and irreverent, she launched into the portrayal of women on popular television shows, a discussion I had never thought would have a place in a university, or anywhere really. It seemed I had taken much for granted. Save Gem, I already was not sure if I had met anyone before so adept at opening my mind.

After a conversation incorporating the whole class, she asked us to divide ourselves into pairs. My recent between-class chat partner caught my eye and gave an inquiring point.

SOON, IT BEING Katia's day off, we ducked into her workplace to dine ourselves. I knew, objectively speaking, I did not need to be spending from my small meal plan. Then again, when and where I used my imaginary dollars was my decision to make.

I found the fish entrée unremarkable but thoroughly enjoyed our conversation. The subjects glided over our intended studies, our high schools (which we both were happy to have behind us), and our former homes. Katia expressed delight in starting over in a new place; my heart throbbed in jealousy, and I changed the subject. I figured this was the type of "getting to know you"-brand speak one should be having at the beginning of college; after all, new friendships had to start somewhere. Then, Katia startled me.

"Do you have a girlfriend?"

"I—" I sputtered. "Did you say...how did you know?" She grinned in triumph.

"I didn't. I just like to ask that instead of the opposite." I nodded, impressed. "Had a feeling, though. My gaydar is impressive. So?"

"So..." It took me a minute. "Oh. Yes, I do. Do you?"

"Not anymore." Katia wiped her mouth with a napkin and crumpled it on her plate. "Left my high school sweetheart for big, bad New Or-leeeens. I knew the long-distance thing wouldn't work out."

My heart thudded. How could I be having a casual conversation with another girl about being gay? Since the end of my stint at CPM, I'd had several male acquaintances who were out, but no one had ever seemed to suspect me, and I hadn't given them clues to help.

Katia went on. "We should go to the bars sometime! Your girl can come too," she added hastily.

I couldn't meet her eyes. "I don't know if that'd be her thing," I improvised. "And besides, I don't have an ID."

Katia tilted her head with an impish smile. "And would it be hard to get one?"

"Probably not," I admitted.

TWO WEEKS LATER, I bought a necklace with a beaded rainbow pattern at an independent bookstore uptown. After paying, I carried it in my hands rather than taking a bag, and I fastened it on as soon as I had stepped outside. Immediately, I felt exposed, but it seemed negligible in the face of the relief flowing through me.

College, I knew, would be my new start, and I wasn't just going to come out; I would *be* out. From that point forward, I decided, I would live as a proud queer woman.

I tried not to think of the inevitable times of exception waiting at home, when I would have to slip the piece of jewelry under my clothes or into a pocket. The necklace was only the beginning, I knew: I could never let my parents catch a glimpse of my pride. They had already been suspicious over my not dating in high school, but this had been mollified by my rigorous studying. They liked an overachiever. So did I, but now, I could achieve something for my own sake, and it might as well start with a cheap necklace.

NOT LONG AFTER, Katia found me an ID that had belonged to a Floridian nurse in her mid-twenties. Katia's own fake identification, she informed me, had been taken care of for years.

By then, I had made several other friends good enough to pass time with, but none intrigued me like her. I could only hope the feeling was mutual. Her being a classmate in Women's Studies, which remained my favorite course, was a bonus, since I often left class still wanting to talk about what we had read. Regardless of my grades, that was a new experience for me.

Katia had been lucky enough to get a dorm room to herself. She had wasted no time in making it hers; the narrow walls were tiled with posters already. She showed me her handiwork one Thursday night, then made us both macaroni and cheese in the hall kitchen as we planned our big night out that weekend.

After we bid farewell, I realized another bus would not arrive for over an hour. I set up my books in the hall lounge to study. I expected to be interrupted constantly by students coming and going, and maybe have to have an awkward conversation with Katia when she noticed me still inside the building, but nobody passed me. Apparently, they all were either out at parties or with friends, or secure in whatever they were doing inside their bedrooms. It left me feeling hollow and isolated.

I knew what my parents would say to Katia's boots on our porch, so we decided on a bar ahead of time. I prepared alone. I told my parents I would be seeing Jill, with whom I had only gotten together twice in the two years previous. The combination of attending different schools and my little scandal at the Academy had put a strain on Jill's and my friendship. I heard her new social circle even included Leigh, who had remained popular as ever since her stitches. Without inhabiting the same sphere, Jill and I had turned out to have little in common. Asha had proven a reliable friend for the weekends for most of tenth grade, until her family had moved back to India. She had been devastated at the prospect of the move but appeared to have flourished, always full of stories about her dates and friends. Our expensive calls and letters hardly seemed worthwhile after some time.

Gem, for once, took more assuaging as I prepared for the bar. "You haven't told me much about your friend, you know," she muttered from the armchair as I dressed. She held a book open in front of her, but I doubted any part of her focused on reading it. Much as she meant to me, I sometimes wished I could have a room to myself.

"What's to tell?" Underwear on, I examined my chest in the mirror and made a face. I would have to start putting some money toward a new bra soon. "Her name's Katia; mom's Russian, father's from Panama; she's from California; thinks she'll major in Women's Studies..."

"None of that says much. Then again, I guess descriptions never mean anything until you meet the person yourself."

"Maybe not." I decided on a basic black tank top. "I do wish you could meet her, though," I added automatically. I felt dishonest saying it and realized some part of me liked the idea of having each of them to myself. *Uh-oh*, I thought; *do I have feelings for Katia?* If I did, surely it was only to be expected. I doubted a person could spend her life loving one individual without even finding others attractive.

As if reading my mind, Gem turned toward me, abandoning her pretense of reading altogether. "Is she cute?"

I nearly jumped. "Katia? I guess. Don't worry, though; she knows about you. I mean...nothing about you, specifically, just that I'm taken."

Gem nodded. "Open-minded as I'm sure your new friends are, I wouldn't assume they're ready to know you're dating the dead."

"Don't say *that*," I sighed, wriggling into my jeans. "I agree, but I wish you wouldn't call yourself dead. It just doesn't fit you." She smiled, but it didn't reach her eyes.

"What'll you do if women ask you to dance?" Gem blurted out, like she had only just thought of it. Of course, I knew her too well to believe it.

"Well...I don't know. Is it okay if I dance with people?"

"So long as it's only friendly, I guess. I mean, use your best judgment. If something doesn't feel right, it's probably not."

I chuckled, studying my reflection and wondering if I should hunt for what little makeup lay somewhere in my room. With a drop in my back pocket, I decided ChapStick was enough. "Those would be good words to live by, I think."

THAT NIGHT, I partook of alcohol for the first time since my fourteenth birthday. My hands were clumsy before I finished my first mixed drink. The bar, which seemed to alternate between neon lights and total blackness, was not at all like I had imagined it. Most of all, it was so loud.

I tried to talk to Katia but found it nearly impossible, so I focused on the other patrons around me. At least half of them were quite a bit older, likely over forty, and the others, who I guessed to be in their twenties, mostly seemed to have come in couples. Then again, they probably took Katia and I to be a couple, so who knew?

The customers indeed seemed to all be women, which, although I knew it was the point, nonetheless surprised me. I suppose I hadn't believed others would respect the wish to keep the establishment for queer women only.

By the time the music increased in volume and people began to drift to the dance floor in couples and groups, I decided I had grown too tipsy to hesitate. I motioned to Katia and hurried onto the polished wood, not quite on the edge but nowhere too visible, and began to sway my hips. Katia took longer to start dancing. I held out my hands, and we took turns twirling each other.

I laughed, though I knew we must have appeared awfully unsophisticated. She leaned forward, and her lips tickled my ear as she said, "I'm going to get another drink." I followed her back to the bar. As she ordered, the longer strands of her boyish haircut fell over her eyes, and when the bartender retreated, I took one in my hands, rubbing the red between two of my fingers.

Katia spoke suddenly. "Don't you have a girlfriend?"

"Yes..."

Katia's eyes caught mine in a hard lock. "Then what are you doing?"

My hand fell away, and with it, it seemed, went the dizzy effects of the drinks. I felt entirely sober, as I now realized I had probably been this entire time. I could blame nothing on inebriation, least of all my burning face. I wanted to deny I had been flirting, but I would have fooled neither of us.

"I'm sorry," I whispered. For one horrible second, I thought I might cry. I had no idea why I wanted to flirt, and maybe do more, and I hated that I would clearly have to confront it. "I guess I'm confused."

Her face softened. She put an arm around me, though our touches were no longer remotely electric. "I understand," she spoke over the music. "But you got to figure it out alone." Staring at my shoes, I nodded. A minute later, I wished her an awkward goodbye, hoping our fledgling friendship would recover, as I stepped back out onto the New Orleans streets for a long solo walk.

BY THE TIME I returned to Dauphine Street, I was no more sorted out. I was, however, significantly past my curfew. I winced as the door creaked then chided my own naïveté. Both my parents, naturally, were waiting just inside the door. Of course I wouldn't get away with having some time to myself. "Where have you been?" Mother hollered, grabbing both of my shoulders.

I pulled away. "At Jill's, I told you." As soon as the words left my mouth, I realized they could easily have phoned Jill's parents. Then again, if they had, it would have been the first thing they said. Maybe, in this respect, luck smiled on me.

Either way, we launched into our tired charade: Mother insisting I could have been brutally murdered, which she described like a daydream; Father's sporadic lean-ins to growl directly into my face and try to shake the terror of God into me; my own murmurs of contrition and innocence.

I had simply lost track of time, I said. What else could I say? After about an hour, I suppose it became clear to Mother and Father that they had nothing to gain by starting a screaming match or making someone sob, respectively. They each announced they were going to bed and ordered me to do the same, with what alternative, I had no idea.

Partly just for the sake of defying their tyranny, and partly to calm myself down before seeing Gem, I sat on the uncomfortable sofa for some time. I stared at the cracks in the wall harboring dozens of roaches, the far edge of the floor that had started needing to be plugged with towels when it stormed. I stared into space until I knew they would be asleep and unrousable.

When I closed my bedroom door, I found Gem jerking awake from yet another time-killing armchair nap. "You were out late, missy."

I pushed my hands through the hair over my sweating scalp. "I know, and I didn't have nearly enough fun to earn the third degree I just got."

"Oh, yeah? You didn't like the bar?"

"I don't know. I just didn't have a good time."

"What were the women like?" Her tone remained careful, and possibly suspicious. This upset me more, because I deserved the suspicion.

"Can't you tell I don't want to talk about it?" I snapped.

Gem, who had begun to stand in greeting, recoiled and sank back into the chair. "Can I ask if you're okay?" she said, with a new edge. I knew full well my girlfriend was not one to be pushed around unfairly and just take it. "Or will that make you angrier at me?"

"I'm not angry; I'm irritated. You know I hate checking in with Mother and Father. I don't want to feel like I have to check in with you too."

"Isn't that part of being in a relationship?" Gem protested. "Letting your partner know if you're not going to be there when they were expecting you, or at least saying why?"

"I guess." I didn't think about what this simple answer implied until Gem jerked back, stricken. "Gem, what?"

"Are you saying, maybe you don't *want* to be in a relationship?"

The words hit me like cold water, unthinkable until she said them out loud. *I must be a terrible person,* I thought, but I didn't quite believe it. My feelings were my own, and I couldn't change them at will. "I...I don't know. I mean, I love you, and I can't imagine my life without you, but...I don't know what I want."

Gem stood up more suddenly than I would have been able to without seeing spots. Arms folded, she turned away from me and stepped toward the opposite corner of the room, but her eyes shone. I realized we had been heading toward this conversation for months. "You say you can't imagine life without me? It's more, for me. You *are* my life, if we even call it that. I don't have the world open to me like you do. I have nothing."

My heart throbbed at the truth in her words, but I resented the emotional manipulation. "I know, Gem, and I hate it—but it's not my fault."

"I didn't say it was!" She kicked the bookcase. "Cassie, I get it. You're old enough to leave the nest now, with all that implies. There's a city of beautiful gay women out there, and you can interact with them beyond these walls, to say nothing of if you leave New Orleans. I just want to contemplate, feelings and drama aside for a minute, what the hell I would *do* if we weren't together."

"It's not up to me, obviously. Wouldn't that be kind of the point?" I grabbed my bag. "Gem, I can't be here right now. I'm confused and overwhelmed. I'm going to stay in the dorms." I wondered if I should call Katia; it would be embarrassing, but perhaps less so than anyone else since I had not met many students.

She followed me down the stairs. "You won't be alone there either, you know."

I pictured my bleak, studious evening, when I'd had the sensation of being in a ghost town. "You'd be surprised."

I opened the front door to the sound of a gleeful voice, alarmingly close. "What did I tell you, Gemmy?"

I stumbled back as a lost child, a girl with matted blonde hair, stepped into the porch light.

But she wasn't just any lost child, I realized. I had seen her many times before.

And after one glance at Gem's face, I finally knew who she was.

# Chapter Seventeen

"DAZE," GEM BREATHED, eyes wide as if she were in a trance. Then, she seemed to shake it off. Once she found her voice again, Gem snarled, "You're not welcome here, and you know it." She reached forward to grab the doorknob, but Daze swung the door all the way outside, holding it out of reach.

"Hold on, now," Daze purred, cutting her eyes at me. "I think the lady of the house here was leaving. Weren't you?"

Gem threw an arm over my torso, forcing both of us farther away as she backed up. "You've been *listening* to us?"

"More than listening. This house is full of windows, as you both seem to forget. I pretty much had a panoramic view for this incident: your last lovers' quarrel." Daze stuck out her lower lip in a parody of sadness. "Took longer than I expected, but didn't I say it would end this way, Gemmy?"

"You don't get to call me that anymore." Gem breathed like she'd run a mile. Even on the few occasions I had seen her get more than a little annoyed, I had never witnessed her like this. "I told you to leave. I told you to go!"

"Wait!" I broke away from Gem's grasp and faced her, feeling myself heat back up. "How long has she been spying on us?"

"Oi, secrets!" Daze flattened herself against the door languidly, reminding me, for some reason, of a panther. "How long have I been here, Gemmy? Tell the nice rebound girlfriend."

"'Rebound gi—'" I cut myself off and hissed, "Let's step outside, because there are people asleep in this house, and I'd like to start yelling!"

"She can't step outside, if I'm not mistaken," Daze shot back, nodding at Gem. "Surely you at least know that." I stared at Gem, trying to ask questions with my eyes. I knew Gem could go as far as the porch. She could share at least a bit of space with Daze if she wanted to, though Daze didn't seem to know it. How many secrets was my girlfriend keeping?

"And don't step out with her either," Gem told me, her voice softening for a second. She glanced back at Daze and added, "We don't know what she's carrying."

"Aw, my violent days are over! You know that. Isn't the lady of the house the one known for knife attacks?"

"Shut up!" I held up my hand to block her and turned back to Gem. "Gem. I want you to tell me *exactly* what's going on here."

She sighed, face crumpled in sorrow. "This is the third time I've seen Daze since her death." I stared and waited for her to continue. "The first was within a year, and I told her to move on because things were finished between us."

Despite myself, I turned to Daze and interrupted. "Why aren't you bound to the jail? Didn't you die there?"

"The jail's gone. There was a little flood a while back, though I wouldn't expect a spring chicken like you to know," Daze spat. "But no, I was never stuck in one place like your girl here. I can pretty much go wherever as long as I stay outside. Maybe it's 'cause I made my noose in the yard; who knows? Ask the man upstairs." Baffled, I turned behind me toward the staircase before I realized what she meant. The motion was not lost on Daze, who snorted.

I reeled back to Gem. "You said, three times. When was the second?"

She looked at her feet. "While you were away."

This took me a minute, too. "At CPM?"

"Yes."

"Did you think to, I don't know, *tell* me at some point?"

"Why?" Gem demanded, her head snapping back up. "I made her promise to leave us alone...even if that apparently didn't mean much to her!" She faced me, but most of her words seemed to be for Daze just as strongly. "She knew I didn't love her anymore. I told her to go off and find her own life, or afterlife. It would've torn you up to know my ex was cruising around the house while you were locked away. Your situation was bad enough!"

"I forgot breakup fights last forever," Daze groaned, snapping our attention back to her. She leaned as close to me as she could without bypassing the doorway, challenge in her steely eyes. "You just run off to your new girl...or boy. Whatever. Gemmy is quite a romantic, but I knew this was coming from day one. A relationship with a human? Tried it. A few times, in fact." She turned back to Gem. "You're not the only one who played around in the decades we were separated. I learned my lesson faster, though. Sooner or later? They leave. They outgrow us. And you, you're bound to a house with controlling, scream-y old people, to boot. What'd you think would happen?"

Gem had begun to cry. "Can't you just leave me, leave us, alone?"

"'Fraid not. I don't meet a lot of people who can see me, and life's awfully boring out there when they can't. You can take stuff from shops, though," Daze added. "You might like that."

Gem turned to me. "Can't we just go back upstairs?"

"Can't hide forever," Daze interjected. "There's no secret society of ghosts or anything. There aren't many of us, I don't think. We're both limited, old friend, you and I. Oh, and by the way, you wouldn't like the shoplifting at all; forget I said it. There's no risk."

Though I knew I shouldn't, I tried to reason with Daze again. "You couldn't be together even if she wanted to! You're stuck outside; she's stuck here. Haven't you realized that?"

She smiled a bit. "I bet we could find a way."

"Oh, no!" Gem exploded. She stomped directly up to the doorway. Her face only reached Daze's chest, probably not as intimidating as she had wanted. "You are not trying to destroy this place!"

"Easy." Daze held up both hands. "If that's what I wanted, I'd have done it years ago. I want you to come to me yourself, once you wise up and realize what we had was the real thing. Never figured you'd be such a slow learner, Gemmy."

"For fuck's sake, stop calling me that!" Gem turned and fled back to the stairs, and I darted out and grabbed the door.

"Do you hate it 'cause it still makes you hot?" Daze shouted after her. Gem stopped short midway up the steps.

"Daze," she whimpered, "it's not that I don't forgive you. It's just, I've moved on."

I slammed and locked the door firmly, though I knew the lock meant nothing, and the two of us retreated to the bedroom, shocked silent.

WHEN I HAD to step outside the house, my danger instincts went on high alert. It marked a change, since before, my load had seemed lighter the farther I went from my parents, so long as I carried pepper spray. I never saw Daze, but I knew this did not mean she wasn't watching.

I grew much more careful with covering windows and my noise level, even when Gem and I had the place to ourselves, or perhaps especially then. Certainly, we did not make love in the following weeks, though I wasn't sure we would have anyway given the depth of my confusion.

In its own way, the situation with Daze allowed me a legitimate distraction from figuring out my feelings. I still was in the first flush of college, but some matters were more imminent than my classes.

Directly after our encounter with Daze, we did not speak at all. I found it difficult to even be near Gem. It had been one matter to know she'd had another love many years before, had experienced the magic of reciprocal passion; I could deal with that. It felt entirely different to look her former lover in the still-youthful face, especially considering how disagreeable Daze was. Besides, I could not help but worry that Gem's failure to mention her other conversations with Daze post-death meant more than she was letting on.

It seemed I should have known someone potentially dangerous had been observing me. It seemed, frankly, like dishonesty. Even if she didn't want to be with Daze anymore, I found it hard to believe Gem had no lingering romantic feelings for her first love. I could not imagine feeling nothing of the sort for Gem, even if we broke up.

And then, of course, I would find myself back in the mental place I most did not want to be in, the one in which I wondered if my time with Gem should be veering toward a close. I knew the house had come to represent a toxic space in my mind, one in which I had little privacy and even less comfort.

Between classes, I wandered through the various dorm halls; other students let me in instinctively, never guessing I did not belong. I peered into others' rooms, some of which were open to show young adults chatting over television or studying in peace, never worrying parents would interrupt with insults or demands. Other doors remained closed, with no one but their owners having access to change that status. Their doors *locked*. With every hall I visited, an ache of want burned in the pit of my stomach, and it had nothing to do with food.

As for Katia, the two of us continued to share notes and lunches, but our friendship had acquired a certain formality. We certainly never hugged anymore, let alone spent time in her room, but I continued to open up to her in our conversations. I did not talk about Gem, but I told her a significant deal about my childhood. It had been pretty strange, I realized. I hedged a little, referring to Chose People Ministries simply as an ex-gay camp. In turn, Katia spoke a little about her idyllic-seeming past; she had come fully out of the closet at the age of fifteen and faced little resistance aside from a few months of parental "Are you sure? Are you *sure*?"

She'd had some trouble at her high school—apparently California was not as uniformly open-minded as I tended to assume—but still, her history seemed strangely easy. I had taken it for granted that every young queer's family would be horrified, and hearing about Katia's laid-back parents and sister nearly brought me to tears.

Sometimes, I still had a painful desire to reach out and kiss Katia. Inevitably, this led to me keeping my distance for a day or two. Other times, I wondered if I actually was attracted to Katia at all. Maybe I simply envied her and craved a larger queer community, one in which I was free to make any sort of connection I chose.

WHEN GEM AND I finally spoke about the matter directly, I did not mince words. I had grown tired of failing to address worrying feelings. "How could you have dated her? She's awful!"

"The years have changed her," Gem sighed. "She's just really, really lonely."

My worst fears seemed on the verge of being confirmed. "Are you defending Daze?"

"No!" she exclaimed. "She's acting out of line, and juvenile, more juvenile than she ever did when we were alive. The fact is, though, she's always been impulsive and aggressive, and probably hasn't learned to meditate the way I have. Before I figured it out, I thought I'd go insane those first few years. Everybody I knew grew up and left, and I couldn't even talk to them."

A flush crept up Gem's face. "When the first new family moved in, I put their stuff in other places just to see if they'd notice, and no one ever did. It was all so boring, I considered vandalism myself. Cassie, before *you* moved in I spent years asleep pretty much nonstop. Daze wants company, and I think she's fixated on me because what she really wants is her life back."

"And you don't?" I questioned softly. "The idea of breaking out to be with her and wreaking havoc like Thelma and Louise again doesn't tempt you?"

"No. I mean, it did once. When Daze first approached me after our deaths, I still was furious at her for basically getting me killed, and I thought killing herself was pretty damn stupid too. I'd already seen my dad give up; knowing my former love sacrificed everything in my honor felt awful. I just wanted to ride out the last of my feelings for her, finish falling out of love, and I did. There's something deeply ruthless in her, and I think it would have eventually torn us apart anyway."

I stayed quiet for a minute, contemplating falling out of love. Had that happened to me with Gem? I wondered how much of our love for each other remained authentic and passionate, and how much was complacent. "She said," I began carefully, "she'd expected me to outgrow you." Gem flinched. "I won't lie and say that didn't trouble me, because it did. But I get the feeling you've outgrown *her*."

"It's true," Gem sighed. "You don't have to grow older to grow up. Look, Cassie, I know you've been wondering about my place in your life now you're becoming an adult, but I just want to remind you of something: I'm not just fifteen. I've been here a while."

I raised an eyebrow. "If that's the case, how old were you when you first seduced me?"

"Cass! You *know* I had trouble—"

"Kidding. I'm kidding. You never did anything untoward. If I recall, I tended to be the aggressive one.

And yes, you're not just fifteen, but at the same time, Gem, you are." We exchanged tender, sad smiles. "And you're right: I don't know what to do about us anymore. I think we've both been stuck in boxes for too long. I'll probably always love you, but...I think I need to escape my past. I have to get out of this household if I ever want to feel healthy again."

Gem's eyes grew misty, but she did not appear surprised in the least. "I understand. I love you too, but if I had the kind of options you have, I can't guarantee I would stay."

I lunged toward the armchair, dizzy with sorrow and relief, and we wrapped each other in an intimate hug. "I know neither of us have a lot of experience to draw from," she murmured against my hair, "but I think this is quite amicable for a breakup." I let out a short burst of laughter at the same moment my eyes spilled over. "Where are you going to go?"

We separated enough to meet each other's eyes. "I'm going to have to see who'll have me as a transfer student first, I guess. I love New Orleans, but too much has happened to me here."

She nodded. "So, uh, would you like me to use a different room?"

I considered. "Nah. Apparently, girls my age share rooms without having sex all the time." Gem pulled the cushion from behind her back and tossed it at me, bringing to mind our years of close friendship. Only then did I remember what this conversation had ostensibly been about. "Gem!"

"Hmm?"

"What are we going to do about Daze?"

Gem sank back in her chair with a sigh. "I wouldn't be surprised if she's already run off to another city. I don't think she would have been as nasty if she really thought I might take her back. Yeah, she might try again eventually, but what *can* we do except ignore her? It helps that this room's on the second floor. I don't think she'd actually hurt you, knowing I love you, and even if she intended to, she couldn't hurt me."

Unexpectedly, I felt a rush of pity for Daze. Imagine being a teenage ghost remembered as a senseless criminal but not even convincing as a threat.

# Chapter Eighteen

ON THE LAST day of so-called dead week, the afternoon before my grandfather's funeral, I stepped through the front door to find Mother waiting for me with a long face, envelope in hand. For the first time in the weeks since my secretive trip to the post office, I had not rushed home to reach the mailbox first. Now, I would pay the price, with the scene I had seen on the horizon all along. The pull of hanging out with my Women's Studies 101 classmates, basking in the simple elation of the new weekend, had proved too much to resist.

Mother waved the large envelope at me in accusation. Before I could harness the defiance that had been bubbling lately, I brightly asked, "I got in, then?"

She threw it on the uneven table, where it slid nearly to the wall. "The University of Arizona? Could you possibly go farther away?"

I gritted my teeth. "Yes, actually. I've already been accepted to schools in California and New York City."

Mother slapped the wooden surface. "Damn it, Cassie! How do you expect us to pay for this, for any of them? Why can't you just stay at Tulane?"

"Because I need to get out." I spoke point-blank. "Aside from a certain year in which I was locked up, I've never been outside of New Orleans except to see your parents on Easter."

"Yes, my parents!" She stood and began rummaging through the kitchen drawers for no reason I could see. "A fine time to pull this stunt! I guess you wanted to leave me as soon as my father did?"

"He wasn't sick yet when I applied!" I retorted. "It takes a little longer, though I guess you wouldn't know. Anyway, I've already filled out info for all the scholarships. I'll go wherever it's cheapest. In fact..." I slid papers out of the open packet and rummaged for a minute before I found what I sought, what I had known all along would be there. "I just got offered the majority of tuition. Tucson it is. I'll work full time year-round for the rest if I need to. Point is, I'm going to make this happen. I'll spend the break making calls, get my records to them, make living arrangements. By mid-January, I'll be gone."

I waited a minute for a response, but she continued to bang through pots, so I made an exit. The topic, of course, would be harped on until the minute I left for good, but just then I wanted nothing more than some time of peace in which to tell Gem.

*Wait.* I stopped short. I did want something else, though not for my own sake. "Mother?" Reluctantly, she turned around. "Have you, um, I was thinking...have you ever thought about...remodeling?"

She stared for a long moment, disdainful and not a little confused. "I will never understand you, Cassandra. Of course not."

I continued up the stairs. It had been a long shot, but worth a try.

AFTER DINNER, AND a long, unnecessary chewing-out by both folks, I spontaneously bussed back to Woolf. I couldn't wait to tell Katia and her neighbors, with whom I had also spent some time, the news. All acted disappointed and said they would miss me, but we left our formal goodbyes for after finals.

Still, Katia gave me a long hug before I headed back home, a hug that spoke of the wasted potential between us. I had no regrets, though. My romantic life would have a fresh start just like my life's other facets.

Heading back downtown, I noticed smoke in the air and wondered if I had forgotten a local celebration. Soon the bus became stalled by fire trucks and police cars, leading my fellow passengers to murmur to one another in speculation and, inevitably, a bit of excitement.

My chest filled up with dread, and I lurched out of my seat and out the door at a desperate run.

I leaped through the sparse side streets of the Ninth Ward and pushed through the tourists milling on Frenchman. Sweat speckled the sidewalk as I ran, and my eyes burned from smoke. Turning onto Dauphine, I froze at the sight I had known in my heart I would find: the house, *our* house, engulfed in flames.

Crowds stood at a safe distance, as if they could see anything crucial from two blocks away. I pushed by strangers' shoulders, their features growing fuzzier. Usually I hated navigating myself through tight groups of people, but this overruled everything.

The fire was huge. It spread so much wider than any I'd seen, it didn't even resemble a fire, more a film over a separate world nothing could touch. It glowed bright as the sun, and I couldn't tell the running shadows inside from the spots in my own eyes.

I ran on toward the white-hot blaze as unidentifiable shapes flared up and disintegrated into its orange bottom.

As my former home grew closer, fingers of flame brushed the blue house to our left. They left singes like black paint but failed to catch.

Three houses away, rough hands hindered my progress. Two young firefighters, a woman and a man in face masks, were holding me back. Their thick gloves stuck to my skin, which had grown slick with sweat. They restrained me as I cried out and reached toward the house as if to hug it into protection. It took a minute to decipher what they were saying. "Are you Cassandra? Or Cassie?"

"Yes! Oh God, is she okay? Was it Daze? Was it her?" I rambled. I continued to stare into the blaze. The light dimmed, spots fading from golds to grays. Every few seconds, another fully covered worker emerged from the smoke. I stared at an upright tangle of metal spikes and curls, trying to match it with my armchair.

"Shh," the man tried to calm me. "It appears someone left the oven on, probably one of your parents. It's the most common cause of domestic fires we see, by far. It's not your fault, and no one was inside."

"But maybe someone was!" I wailed, collapsing on the ground. I had no way to explain and no means with which to get near the building aflame. I disappeared inside myself, paralyzed at the idea of a universe without Gem. There was too much we didn't know about the ghostly rules of existence. I had not kept her safe.

When the charred remains of the French Victorian architecture showed no sparks, numerous authorities tried to escort me away, but I wrestled free and sprinted into the ashes and scraps of wall. "Gem!" I screamed, darting through the wreck.

"Yeah?"

I whirled around, and there she was. My Gem.

She stood across the street in an empty grass lot, as beautiful and whole as I'd ever seen her. She grinned among the weeds, positively glowing, though the fire had gone. Nonchalantly, she brushed a stray ash from her Boy Scout shirt as I sprinted toward her, not caring who might see. Everyone would write off my actions as shock, or possibly think the smoke had made me incoherent.

"You're okay," I whispered, my hands around her shoulders.

"Better," she answered, putting her arms around me as well. "I'm free."

"We both are." My throat thickened with tears. "This is exactly what I would have wanted for you, Gem. I don't care about anything else in the house. I wanted to give you freedom for Christmas, but I didn't know how." *And this is so much more appropriate than my half-baked remodeling idea,* I added silently.

"Guess your mom finally caught that arson bug my presence has been rumored to inspire."

"Subconsciously, huh? How about that." We studied each other in the hazy light. I knew I had to look hard, because Gem would no longer be bound to Dauphine Street, to my bedroom walls, or to me. I knew she would leave, and I wanted her to go, but I knew I would miss her like anything.

Simultaneously, we leaned in for a comforting kiss. It was the first time we had kissed in months, and I knew it would also be the last.

After we finally let go of each other, there was no need to say goodbye. We gazed into each other's eyes one more time, and then we turned away. I forced myself to focus on the remains of the house instead of at her retreating back. I struggled not to look at first, but in the face of the liberating, inexplicable beauty of the wreckage, I felt awash with contentment.

For the first time, I wondered if there *was* some grand story to all our messy lives.

# Epilogue

MY FIRST WINTER in Tucson proved as new and exciting as I had expected. It was especially relaxing compared to having shared a motel with my parents for finals week, and the extended stay with my grandmother until my housing assignment had come through. By the time I managed to get on a train west, I had been subjected to predictable theories about how the accident had actually been *my* fault, how the stress of my transferring news had been too much for my mother at such a time...

Now, aside from the irritation of an occasional phone call, it was all behind me.

Even before my classes began, I managed to make friends under the persistent Arizona sun. I spent as much time as possible in the artistic spots around town, with on-campus clubs, and in my dorm hall of similarly green freshmen. As I'd hoped, most treated my sexuality as a non-issue, because I stepped onto the University campus openly queer. I went on several dates in my first few months, but no major romance developed. It was just as well. It would take a special woman, and a special commitment, to fully understand my history.

I tried not to consider the possibility that Gem had found and gotten back together with Daze. I couldn't see them reuniting forever, but maybe for a night. I couldn't blame her if she had. Despite Daze's instability, I understood the seduction of the familiar, especially when both of them had so few others with whom to connect. When I wondered about Gem, understandably often despite my new life, I reminded myself I no longer held sway over her choices. I had two simple hopes for her: that she was well, and that she thought of me fondly.

On the Friday I received the postcard, my mind burst with plans: about studies, about which clubs to hit, about where to spend part of my first paycheck from the coffeehouse before I put most away like the responsible soul I was. For the last, I presently leaned toward a cozy independent bookshop with a feminist bent I had recently discovered.

When I saw the photo of the New York skyline, though, everything else left my mind. I flipped the card over to familiar wobbly handwriting, and my heart rose.

*Dearest Cassie,*

*It took some time to get a hold of your new address, and more to contemplate whether it would be appropriate to write you at all. In the end, care and plain curiosity won out, because I can't imagine not at least finding out if you're okay, and letting you know where in the world I am.*

*As you can see, I'm taking a bite out of the Big Apple, but I've traveled a lot already. I seem to have no binding barriers anymore. Turns out, it's easy to board planes when no one can see you. Well, almost: I've met two other humans so far who can see me! The first, a young man, knows Daze and says she's living with, or near, her new ghost girlfriend in Chicago. I met the other in Florida, but you already know her...her name is Palace! She's a cool girl and a major radical political force in her community.*

*Overall, I'm loving life, though of course I miss you. Is sleepaway college all that you'd hoped? I wish you every happiness.*

*Gem*


I wiped a stray tear and revised my weekend plan to include a letter to Gem. I would tell her I was happy and fulfilled, not revealing too much but writing with the intimacy we would probably always have with each other.

I put the postcard in my jean pocket and went on my way, smiling at the setting sun.

# Acknowledgements

Big thanks to Raevyn, Elizabeth, Natasha, and the other folks at NineStar Press for helping me share Cassie's story. Other thanks go to #kisspitch, Finishing Line Press, NaNoWriMo, AWP, the Kentucky Women Writers Conference, the Cambridge Writers' Workshop, New Orleans Public Library, and every locale or publication that has hosted me and embraced my words.

Special gratitude to my friends and dear ones, including in-laws extraordinaire Brenda and Kevin. Thanks to Ian, who provided enormous support during the writing of this book.

And, as always, a monumental thank you to Kelsey.

# About the Author

Deb Jannerson is the author of the acclaimed poetry collections *Rabbit Rabbit* (Finishing Line Press, 2016) and *Thanks for Nothing* (Finishing Line Press, 2018), available wherever books are sold. *The Women of Dauphine* is her debut YA novel. Jannerson won the 2017 So to Speak Nonfiction Award for "Scarring," a short memoir about queer intimacy and PTSD; the 2018 Flexible Persona Editors' Prize for "Cut," a piece of flash fiction about gruesome work injuries; and a Two Sisters contest for "The Change," a story about switching bodies with her cat. "Cut" was also nominated for a Pushcart Prize. More than one hundred of her pieces have been featured in anthologies and magazines, including viral articles for *Bitch*. She lives in New Orleans with her wife and pets.

Email: dpjannerson@gmail.com

Facebook: www.facebook.com/DebJannersonWrites

Twitter: @DebJannerson

Website: www.debjannerson.com

# Also Available from NineStar Press

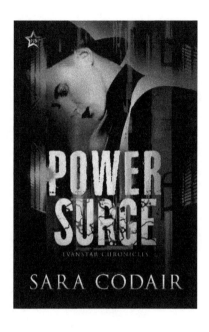

## Connect with NineStar Press

www.ninestarpress.com

www.facebook.com/ninestarpress

www.facebook.com/groups/NineStarNiche

www.twitter.com/ninestarpress

www.tumblr.com/blog/ninestarpress